*I*nside the tack room, Danielle tried not to hear the sound of Redman's hoofs on the gangplank as he was loaded into the van. Grief and hot anger rushed through her. She couldn't believe this was actually happening. Then came the rumble of the van's motor and the grinding of gears.

Redman was gone. Who knew when she'd ever see her beloved horse again?

And there was nothing she could do about it.

The BLACK STALLION SERIES

BOOKS BY WALTER FARLEY

The Black Stallion
The Black Stallion Returns
Son of the Black Stallion
The Island Stallion
The Black Stallion and Satan
The Black Stallion's Blood Bay Colt
The Island Stallion's Fury
The Black Stallion's Filly
The Black Stallion Revolts
The Black Stallion's Sulky Colt
The Island Stallion Races
The Black Stallion's Courage
The Black Stallion Mystery
The Horse-Tamer
The Black Stallion and Flame
Man o' War
The Black Stallion Challenged!
The Black Stallion's Ghost
The Black Stallion and the Girl
The Black Stallion Legend
The Young Black Stallion (with Steven Farley)

BOOKS BY STEVEN FARLEY

The Black Stallion's Shadow
The Black Stallion's Steeplechaser

YOUNG BLACK STALLION

1

The Promise

Steven Farley

Random House ⌂ New York

For Tulipani

Copyright © 1998 by Steven Farley
Cover art copyright © 1998 by Joanie Schwartz
Horse image on cover copyright © Benn Mitchell/
The Image Bank 1998

www.randomhouse.com/kids
Library of Congress Catalog Card Number: 98-066867
ISBN: 0-679-89141-2—ISBN: 0-679-99141-7 (lib. bdg.)
RL: 4.5

Printed in the United States of America
10 9 8 7 6 5 4 3 2 1

Contents

Riding Buddies

Danielle Conners inhaled the familiar smells of hay and horses as she entered the barn. In the corner stall, her horse, Redman, was nosing around his feed trough, licking up the last few grains of his supper.

"Good boy," Danielle called. She opened the screened top half of the stall door and reached in to undo the latch. As she walked inside the stall, she slipped her hand into her jacket pocket and pulled out a carrot. "I brought you a treat."

Redman's ears pricked at the sound of breaking carrot. He turned his big, soulful eyes to Danielle. She held out her hand, and he greedily snatched up a piece of carrot, then stood by, waiting for another. When Danielle shook her head, Redman started nudging her pockets with his muzzle, looking for more treats.

"Hang on just a second there, mister," she said,

pocketing the other half of the carrot. "The rest is for later."

Redman gave a grouchy snort and thrashed his tail. Danielle chuckled. "Faker," she scolded. She reached up to scratch behind his ears. Redman pressed his head into her chest, whuffling softly.

Redman was a big, gentle butterball of a horse, a nine-year-old gelding. His breeding had always been something of a mystery, but there could be no question that he was part pinto, what some people called a "paint" horse. His coat was dark red, marked with splotches of white that looked as if he'd just leaned up against something covered with fresh white paint. Most of his face was white except for a dark red spot around his eye. Danielle thought the spot masking his left eye made him look like a pirate wearing an eye patch.

Ducking into the tack room, Danielle grabbed Redman's bridle from a peg on the wall. The feel of the soft leather tack, light and supple in her hands, made her even more eager to hit the trail for her afternoon ride.

"Okay, Reddy," she called. "Let's get going."

Redman followed her down the aisle. A minute later, she had him all saddled up and ready to go. She led him from the barn, through the paddock and out the front gate. Carefully closing the gate behind her, she took a few short, quick steps and hopped up into the saddle. Redman steadied him-self as she settled into her seat. Then Danielle nudged him into a slow, ambling walk.

Crossing the driveway, they passed the Coop, an old chicken coop her dad had converted into a guesthouse. A moment later, they were starting along the path that ran along the bottom edge of the lower pasture. They turned left when they reached the fence bordering Mr. Wiggins's cow field, then followed the gently sloping trail that led between their neighbor's property and the two fenced-in pastures belonging to Danielle's family.

As they made their way along the corridor between the two fences, someone over at Mr. Wiggins's barn started up a tractor. Redman shied at the sudden noise, bolting ahead with a snort. With fencing on either side of the path, there was no place he could go but straight ahead.

"Easy, guy. Easy," Danielle cooed. She let Redman run for a moment or two before coaxing him to a walk again.

Soon they reached the far end of the upper pas-ture. Giving the reins a gentle cross-pull, Danielle told Redman "whoa" and turned to look back down the gentle slope. Cloud shadows drifted across the wide fields of grass as a soft wind whispered by. She gazed out over the sea-green pastures and beyond, to the paddock and barn and the cozy little farmhouse that had been her home ever since she could remember. It was her private little kingdom.

Yeah, whispered a voice inside her head, *but for how much longer?* The family farm was up for sale. Ol' Mrs. What's-Her-Face from the real estate office was still bringing prospective buyers over to see the house every few days. Danielle sighed. For a while she'd thought her mom might change her mind about selling the farm and moving to the Coast. If business would just pick up at the advertising agency where her mom worked, she wouldn't feel so desperate about their money situation. Or maybe one of her dad's new songs would finally hit the charts.

Danielle wiggled into a more comfortable position in the saddle and tried to forget about all those things. On a pretty day like this, it seemed silly to let such dreary thoughts ruin everything. She had a much better plan in mind than worrying over things she couldn't do anything about.

Almost every day after school, or whenever they could get away with it, Danielle and Julie Burke, her neighbor and saddle partner, went riding somewhere. Today they had planned to meet at a spot where the trail branched off to Deer Town Gulch, about halfway between their two homes.

But when she and Redman arrived at the fork, Danielle saw no sign of Julie. She dismounted, and Redman immediately began munching a favorite patch of grass. Danielle flopped down on the ground. As she waited for her friend, she gazed up at the black silhouettes of the treetops swaying in the breeze and thought about her dad, who was off on tour with his band. Danielle wondered how long it would be before he came home again.

A few minutes later, Redman whinnied and Danielle heard hoofbeats clip-clopping up the trail. She sat up quickly and saw Julie and her gray Arabian mare, Calamity, trotting toward her. Julie was twelve and a half, almost the same age as Danielle. Her hair was wavy, black, and cut short with bangs, unlike Danielle's, which was straight, blond, and shoulder length. The two of them were dressed almost identically in their uniform of jeans, cowboy boots, and baggy plaid work shirts.

Julie was Danielle's best friend—after Redman. Julie loved to go tramping around the backcountry on horseback, just like Danielle. Between the two of them, they knew every trail and open field for miles around Wishing Wells.

"Hey!" Julie called, waving.

"What took you so long?" Danielle asked. "I almost fell asleep."

"I had to help my mom bring in the laundry and stuff."

Danielle jumped to her feet and called Redman to her. "We'd better get going if you still want to check out that construction site. Maybe we'll get lucky and find some more shark's teeth."

Julie nodded. "Sure. We still have time."

Danielle climbed back up into the saddle. Soon the two girls and their horses were headed to the spot a couple of miles away where the state was building a new power line. Last week they'd found handfuls of petrified prehistoric shark's teeth in the dirt dug up by the bulldozers.

A narrow trail led the way to the site, winding between the tall pines that bordered South Wind and Overton Bloodstock, two large Thoroughbred farms. Danielle and Julie stopped awhile to watch the exercise riders who were galloping a pair of Thoroughbreds at South Wind's half-mile training track.

Danielle gazed at them and sighed. "Can you imagine getting paid to ride horses?"

Julie smiled. "Sounds like my kind of job."

"Are you still going to try to work at Overton?"

Julie nodded. "When I get old enough."

Danielle turned to her friend. "Your dad wouldn't mind?" she asked. Julie's dad worked at Overton as a stable manager in charge of weanlings and yearlings.

"I don't think so," Julie said. "As long as I kept up with my schoolwork."

"Sounds fair, I guess."

"And I'd have to work my way up, just like anyone else, mucking stalls and walking hots." Julie shifted her gaze to some far-off place on the horizon. "Mom's a different story, though. I don't know if she'd go for it."

Danielle nodded. "I know what you mean. Every time I hint around about getting a job as an exercise rider, my mom starts talking about how dangerous it is. She always says that so-and-so's daughter broke her arm or someone else sprained his ankle and blah-blah-blah."

"Moms are all the same." Julie sighed.

Someone who loved horses, Danielle thought as another horse and rider galloped by, *couldn't ask for much more than to live around here.* Ocala, Florida, practically had more horses than people. It was one of the most important regions in the whole world for breeding and raising racehorses. That was because there were only three places in the world that grew the bluegrass that Thoroughbreds thrived on— Kentucky, Ireland, and right here in Marion County.

All kinds of horse farms surrounded Ocala, and not just Thoroughbred farms. You could find horses of practically every breed in Central Florida, from Arabians to Paso Finos to quarter horses. There were plenty of places to ride around Wishing Wells, the town where Danielle and her family lived.

The two girls hit the trail again. "Your mom's right, you know," Julie said after a moment.

"Yeah?" Danielle asked. "Says who?"

"My dad, for one. And Amy Pitcher. Her big sister is riding two-year-olds at Overton. Amy says her sister has been hobbling around on a twisted ankle for weeks. And the last time I went to Overton I saw at least three people with casts on their arms."

Danielle shrugged. "Can't be much more dangerous than delivering pizza or working at the Quick Mart. If you take one of those jobs, you risk getting robbed or something. How old do you have to be to work at a place like South Wind?"

"Fourteen, I think."

Fourteen sure seemed like a long way away to Danielle, even though it really wasn't far off at all.

"It's nice to be out here, isn't it?" Danielle said. "School was such a drag today. Can you believe all the homework Mrs. Williams stuck us with?"

Julie shrugged. "It's not so bad."

"I hate geometry," Danielle said.

"Come on, that stuff's easy. I'll help you if you want."

Danielle shook her head. "No thanks." It should not have surprised her that Julie didn't mind the extra work. Her friend was smart, the sort of person who never forgot a word that was said over hours of conversation. Besides being such a brain, Julie was pretty, in a cowgirlish sort of way. Before they started hanging out together, Danielle had thought Julie was a bit of a snob. Once she got to know her, though, through their mutual love of horses, she realized that what she'd thought was Julie's air of superiority was really just shyness.

Ahead of them, the trail through the pines opened onto a green field. Danielle and Julie cantered their horses past a cluster of oaks, some low palm trees, and palmetto bushes.

Danielle rode seat-of-the-pants Western-style, all hands and shoulders. Julie rode English-style, always conscious of her position in the saddle. She controlled every move with pinpoint pressure from her knees and thighs.

Julie leaned forward and playfully grabbed a handful of her horse's mane. "Want to race, Hot Stuff?"

Danielle glanced back at Julie and made a noise like a race car revving up its engine. Julie laughed. She laughed a lot, which was another thing that Danielle really liked about her. She made Danielle feel comfortable, and her sometimes cynical jokes were often directed at herself.

A mischievous glint sparkled in Julie's eyes as she glanced down at Redman. "The old guy's not going to have a heart attack on us, is he?" she teased.

Danielle gathered up her reins. *"Rummm... Rummm..."*

"Okay, then," Julie said. "On three. One... Two... Hey!" she cried as Redman suddenly bolted forward.

"I couldn't stop him," Danielle called over her shoulder.

They pushed their horses to a gallop for a quarter-mile. Then Calamity suddenly decided she'd had enough and pulled up short. Julie seemed to be half expecting it. She threw her weight back on Calamity's hindquarters and collected the mare, bringing Calamity quickly into balance again.

"Give me a break, Calamity," said Julie, her voice firm but gentle. "Why do you have to be this way all the time? I always tell everyone you're so good. You're making a liar out of me."

Redman and Danielle came to a stop and waited. The big paint lowered his long neck to the ground and began munching grass until Calamity strolled over to join him. Redman lifted his head and the two horses touched their noses together for a moment or two, as if sharing a secret.

Danielle chuckled. "Might as well give it up, Julie. Just face it. That bubble-headed mare of yours will never be in the same class as good ol' Reddy."

"Thank heavens for that," Julie quipped.

A few minutes later, the girls and their horses reached the power line. There wasn't much to see: just some holes in the ground, a high metal tower, a white trailer, a bulldozer, and a big pile of dirt. But that didn't matter. The real attraction for Danielle and Julie was the treasure they might find among the rocks and shells in the mounds of dirt that had been churned up by the bulldozers.

A yellow ribbon with DO NOT CROSS printed on it marked the perimeter of the construction area. Danielle jumped off Redman and ducked under the ribbon as if it wasn't there.

"Smart, Danielle," Julie called. "You want to get arrested for trespassing?"

Danielle shrugged. "It'll be okay. We're not hurting anything."

Julie gazed toward the bulldozer parked beside one of the metal towers. "It might be dangerous or something. Don't you see that guy in the Jeep over there?"

Danielle glanced in the direction her friend was looking. Sure enough, a man was sitting in the vehicle, staring straight at them. Danielle back-stepped to the yellow ribbon. "Doesn't look like they've turned over much more dirt here anyway," she said, ducking under the ribbon again.

The girls mounted up and started home through the tunnel of pines. When they reached the ridge overlooking her family's farm, Danielle spotted a shiny red Cadillac parked in the driveway. It belonged to that creepy realtor lady. She suddenly remembered her mom telling her that some potential buyers would be stopping by that afternoon.

Julie recognized the car, too. "Maybe your mom will change her mind about moving."

"I wish," Danielle said with a sigh. "She still thinks she can get a better job on the Coast."

"Too bad. Have many people been by to look at your house so far?" Julie asked sympathetically.

"A few. But still no buyers, luckily. You wouldn't believe all the clean-up frenzies we have to go through every time old Mrs. What's-Her-Face is about to bring someone by. You'd think the president was coming over to eat dinner off the kitchen floor."

Julie laughed.

"Nobody will buy it, I bet," Danielle said hopefully. "Look how long the Lesters' place has been for sale. Years. And Linda Harvey's, too. It's not like people are dying to move here to Wishing Wells. There aren't many jobs."

"What does your dad say?" Julie asked.

Danielle shrugged. "He always backs up my mom, no matter what. And I think he feels bad he hasn't been making much money lately."

"I can't believe you guys might really just pack up and go."

"Me, neither," Danielle said in a small voice.

"But what if you *do* move to the Coast?" Julie

asked. "What about Redman? Will he go, too?"

Danielle leaned forward and laid her head against Redman's neck. "Sure. We'll figure something out, won't we, guy?" She sat up in her saddle again and gazed out across the fields to the house.

"There's always a stall in our barn, you know," Julie offered.

"Thanks, Jule. I don't know what your dad would say about that, though. Redman isn't exactly a weanling or yearling like the rest of the horses in that barn. And he eats a lot."

Julie shrugged. "Hey, Dad might go for it. Anyway, I'll ask him if you want."

Danielle smiled at her friend, but she couldn't help feeling sad and worried inside.

"Well, I sure hope your mom changes her mind about moving," Julie said. "I'd hate to lose my best riding buddy."

"Let's just not think about it, okay?" Danielle said firmly. "It isn't going to happen."

ℭ CHAPTER TWO ℭ

Unwelcome Visitors

The sky was already beginning to turn a hazy purple in the west. It would be a nice sunset, Danielle thought. Over the horizon, faint streaks of silvery clouds looked like scrawled handwriting in the sky. Danielle imagined it saying "Wishing Wells," just like that big "Hollywood" sign in the California hills.

"I'd better get home," said Julie. She leaned forward and slapped palms with Danielle. "See ya at school tomorrow."

"See ya," Danielle replied.

Julie nudged Calamity down the trail, following the ridge toward her house. The elegant gray mare threw back her head and snorted a burst of air through her wide nostrils.

Danielle walked Redman to the upper pasture gate, then opened and closed it behind them. Redman dawdled, more interested in the world beyond the pasture fence than in returning to the barn. Danielle wasn't so eager to get home herself. The realtor lady was the biggest phony she'd ever met. She had a canned Southern accent that made Danielle want to throw up, especially when she called Danielle names like "Sugar Lump" and "Honey Pie." A permanent smile seemed ironed onto the woman's pasty white face, and her eyes were positively reptilian. She made Danielle think of a hungry mother alligator eyeing her children and weighing the pros and cons of eating them for dinner.

Danielle let her legs hang loose outside the stirrups as Redman moved slowly ahead. After a while she started to hum a song that her dad had written. There were some really high notes in it, and she was a little off pitch. Redman didn't seem to mind. He bobbed his head and nickered as they made their way home.

When the gently rolling pastureland began to flatten out, Danielle pushed Redman into a trot. With a whinny, the stocky paint took off, his hoofbeats padding lazily through the grass. He whinnied again when he neared the familiar paddocks and barn.

Even at such an easy gait, Danielle felt that wonderfully familiar feeling of power that riding Redman always gave her. Sure, she'd ridden faster horses and more expensive, well-bred ones. She'd even ridden a stakes-winning mare who'd been reschooled for pleasure riding when she and her dad were visiting a friend of his at a small Thoroughbred farm last year. And she'd ridden Arabians and quarter horses, too. But to Danielle, none of them could compare with Redman.

It wasn't just because he was hers, or that they had grown up together, although those things did mean a lot. There was something unique about Redman, something that made him unlike any other horse she'd ever saddled.

Riding Redman was like being part of something bigger than the two of them, something really special. Often that feeling would stick with her for hours after a ride, making the world seem like a pretty terrific place. The best part was always having another ride on Redman to look forward to.

She'd tried to explain to people the way she felt about her horse. But whenever she did, the words always came out sounding stupid or silly. The only person who really understood was her dad. It was sort of the way he felt about his favorite old six-string guitar, the one he said had a tone unlike any other. If the house was burning down and her dad could save only one thing besides his family, that dented old guitar would be it.

Danielle dismounted outside the barn. It was a narrow, sun-bleached white building with green trim, not much more than a long shed with a low, peaked roof. There was a center aisle with four box stalls on one side. On the other side were two stalls, a large tack room with a small table and a couple of chairs in one corner, and an alcove that held feed and tools.

Danielle walked her horse into the barn and took off his saddle and tack. When Redman nuzzled her hand, she took a peppermint candy from her pocket, unwrapped it, and handed it to him. "Okay, okay. I know you're not supposed to have these, but…"

As Redman happily crunched up his candy, she unwrapped another peppermint for herself and popped it into her mouth. "Fair's fair," she said. "One for you, one for me." The big paint har-rumphed and tossed his head.

"What are *you* complaining about?" Danielle scolded. "I had to go to school today, not you. I wish I could just run around in a field and play all the time like you."

Collecting buckets, brushes, and sponges from the alcove, she led Redman outside again. She filled the buckets from the wall faucet and gave him a good washing and sponge bath. Then she walked him around the barn a few times so he could dry off.

After their fifth or sixth lap of the barn, Danielle saw her mom come out through the porch door. With her were the realtor lady and two men. One was about her dad's age, a tall string bean of a guy wearing a wide-brimmed black cowboy hat. The other man was much younger, maybe eighteen or nineteen, with red hair. He was at least a foot shorter than the man in the cowboy hat. Danielle squinted. Good-looking, too. And by the way the realtor lady and her mom were talking with the redheaded guy, it seemed as if he was the one in charge.

The visitors shook hands with Mrs. Conners and then got into the realtor lady's Cadillac. As they drove off, Danielle's mom gazed after the car awhile. Then she reached up to clang the dinner bell, giving the signal that supper was ready. At the sound of the bell, Danielle's stomach suddenly started grumbling. She congratulated herself on having avoided another encounter with the realtor lady. It was safe to go inside the house now.

Danielle quickly finished grooming Redman, put away the combs and brushes, settled the paint into his stall, and headed for the house. As she ran up the porch steps, she could smell dinner. Spaghetti. She rushed down the hall to the bathroom to wash her hands. She hadn't been there more than a minute when she heard her older brother, Dylan, clomping down the hall. "C'mon, Danielle," he called, banging on the bathroom door. "Mind if I get in there some time this century?"

Danielle finished drying her hands and opened the door. "All yours."

"About time," Dylan said as he brushed past her. "Phew. You smell like a barn."

Danielle made a face at her brother's back. His reddish-blond hair was streaked with patches of black. It looked as if machine oil had leaked on him.

Dylan loved mechanical things. He spent endless hours tearing them apart, hunting odd-looking gears and sprockets. The toolshed was cluttered with butchered sewing machines, adding machines, old radios, telephones, and other junk. His latest project was dismantling a box stapler he'd found in town the weekend before. Danielle would never understand his fascination for that stuff. Maybe it was some kind of a guy thing.

"Nice hair, Dylan," Danielle said. "You look like a skunk."

"Shut up," Dylan snarled, slamming the door behind him.

"Want us to bring you your dinner in there?" Danielle kidded. "You could stay in there forever."

"Mind your own business, will you, Miss Cow Pie?"

Danielle chuckled to herself. Despite their bickering, she and her brother were very close. As much as they might tease each other, Dylan would not tolerate anyone else's saying a word against Danielle.

She felt the same way about him. Dylan was tall for fifteen, nearly six feet, and skinny. His reddish-blond hair stuck out in places, all over the top of his head. When they weren't smudged with grease and grime, his cheeks were lightly spotted with freckles.

As the three of them sat down at the dinner table, Danielle could tell by the distracted expression on her mother's face that something was up. "You won't believe who that was with Mrs. Mack this afternoon," Mrs. Conners said, spooning spaghetti sauce onto her pasta. "Alec Ramsay. You know, the famous jockey."

Danielle's mouth dropped open. She knew all about Alec Ramsay and his fantastic stallion called the Black. The Black was about the most famous racehorse in the whole world.

"Well," Mrs. Conners went on, "Alec brought the Black and a string of other horses to South Wind for the winter. He's looking for a place to stay and also to stable a few more horses."

"Who was the other guy?" Danielle asked, twisting up a forkful of spaghetti.

"That was Billy Spicer, one of the trainers over at South Wind," Mrs. Conners told her. "Anyway, Alec really seems to like it here, especially since it's so close to South Wind."

Dylan didn't seem to be paying much attention to what their mother was saying. He was intent on shaking as much cheese onto his spaghetti as possible. But Danielle had forgotten her food completely. As a rule she didn't like to meet or have anything to do with anyone who came to look at the house. It was hard to see those people as anything more than strangers trying to take her home away. But it wasn't every day you had a Kentucky Derby winner walking around inside your house.

"For someone so young, that Alec Ramsay sure seems as if he knows what he wants," Mrs. Conners continued. "He spent most of his time checking over the barn and paddocks, but he looked around the house and the Coop, too. He seemed impressed." Her voice softened a bit. "This might be it, kids. I just have a feeling. Our chance to make the big move."

"I think we've heard *that* somewhere before," said Dylan as he forked up a glob of noodles. He was right, Danielle thought. It seemed as if every person who came to look at the house said they were interested, but so far no one had made a serious offer.

"Well, I don't know, honey," Mrs. Conners said. "He sounded serious. And he's in a hurry to find a place."

Danielle pushed away her plate. "I still don't understand why you think we have to leave Wishing Wells. Don't you trust Dad? One of his new songs is definitely going to make it big. They're all great."

Mrs. Conners sighed. "Of course I trust your dad, Danielle. But you know how hard it's been for us this past year. The bank doesn't care if your father writes top country-western hits or cleans toilets for a living. They just want their money."

Danielle never gave up an argument easily. "But what about…" she began.

Mrs. Conners held up one hand and narrowed her eyes. That was a familiar signal to Danielle that the subject was no longer up for discussion. "Alec is coming back tomorrow to take another look around," she said. "And I want both of you kids to meet him. He doesn't act like a big shot or anything, Danielle. He's really nice. I bet you might even get a chance to see the Black sometime if you ask."

Danielle began to feel a little dizzy. Everything was happening so quickly. Meeting the world's most famous racehorse would be a dream come true. She'd seen him race on TV, and she'd heard plenty of stories about him. But to actually see the Black in the flesh…*Wow!*

On the other hand, what if Alec Ramsay really did buy their farm? Then her family would certainly be leaving Wishing Wells, and all of their lives would totally change.

Forever.

ᔅ CHAPTER THREE ᔆ

The Black's Colt

When Danielle and Dylan arrived home from school the next day, their mom met them on the porch. She looked very happy. "Guess what? He's already been here. He's coming back later. And he wants to make a deal."

Danielle froze. "Alec Ramsay?"

"Of course Alec Ramsay," her mother said. "Isn't that exciting? Didn't I tell you I had a good feeling about this?"

"Just like that? He's not just coming by to take another look?"

"No, honey. Didn't you hear anything I said?"

Danielle shook her head, feeling shell-shocked.

"Okay, then," her mom said gently. She had a huge smile on her face. "Here it is, one more time. Alec talked things over with Henry Dailey, the head trainer at Hopeful Farm. That's the Ramsay family's stable in upstate New York. And Mr. Dailey decided

23

that having their own base in Ocala would cut down on expenses at South Wind. They want to make a deal right away."

"Are you serious?" Danielle was still stunned.

"I've never been more serious, hon. The way I see it, we'll probably take a month or so to get ourselves organized for the move to the Coast," their mother went on, her words tumbling out faster and faster. "Meanwhile, Alec can stay in the cottage while he's working with his horses. He wants to get started immediately. That's part of the deal. A few weeks from now we'll all be at the beach. Isn't that great, kids? Pretty exciting, huh?" Mrs. Conners placed one reassuring hand on Danielle's shoulder and the other on Dylan's.

Danielle looked at her brother. He seemed shocked, too.

No one spoke for a minute. Danielle searched for words, but they wouldn't come out. When she finally found them, she could hear a hint of panic in her voice. "A month?" she practically squeaked. "Just like that?"

"Give it a break, Danielle," said Dylan, trying to be Mr. Cool. "We don't have to go through this whole stupid thing again, do we? It's a done deal." He adjusted the baseball cap on his head. "Great news, Mom." He swaggered out to the toolshed, trying to look tough. Danielle wasn't fooled a bit. She knew her brother was just as upset as she was. Well, almost.

Mrs. Conners turned back to Danielle. "Honey…"

Danielle bit back tears, barely able to hold in all the sadness and anger she felt. This was their home. It belonged to *them*, not the bank, not even some famous jockey from up North.

"It'll be fun on the Coast, sweetie, you'll see," her mother said.

"Sure, Mom," said Danielle, trying to be brave for her mom's sake. Deep down, her mom probably felt awful about leaving Wishing Wells, too. But for some reason, this was the way things had to be.

A whinny from the paddock made both of them turn. Redman was stretching his head up above the four-rail-high fence, waiting for Danielle.

"Go on, hon," Mrs. Conners told her. "But it'll be homework time straight after dinner. And please don't get in the way when Alec Ramsay gets here. I know you'll want to meet him, but he's supposed to be bringing some of the horses over anytime. He didn't say so, but I think he's stuck for a place to keep them, so I told him it was okay. And I know I don't have to tell you to be courteous and behave yourself, no matter how you're feeling right now."

"Sure, Mom," Danielle said. Then she turned and ran toward the paddock. She still felt as if none of this was really happening. How could her mom act so casual about leaving the only home Danielle had ever known? And her mom had grown up here, too. Why would living on the Coast be so much better than living here? Was a better job and making more money really that important?

Danielle fought back tears as she ran across the driveway. She knew her mom's reasons. How many times had she heard them?

Her mom was a graphic designer for a local advertising and public relations firm. She worked at home a lot, which was great, but the pay was lousy. She was good with computers and had already designed Web pages for companies posting on the Internet. She wanted to learn more about on-line services and technology. By living on the Coast, where there were more people and opportunities, she figured she could better her skills and get ahead faster.

Great, Danielle thought. *But what about me?* And her mom hadn't said anything about Redman. Where could they find a place for him on the Coast? Alec Ramsay had practically moved in already, and they didn't even have a place lined up for their own family to stay yet.

Redman saw her coming. He whinnied again anxiously and began pacing back and forth by the paddock gate. Danielle threw her arms around the big paint's neck and buried her head in his red mane. Hot tears finally began to flow from the corners of her eyes. At least she didn't have to be brave now. Redman understood.

On the way home from school, Julie had told Danielle she had to help her dad at the farm that afternoon. That meant Danielle and Redman were on their own. It was just as well, Danielle thought. She needed to be alone with her horse.

Redman stood still, always the gentleman, as Danielle slipped on his saddle and bridle. "Let's go, boy," Danielle said. "You and I are out of here."

Soon the two of them were topping the ridge above the upper pasture. After that they followed a grassy trail down to a black water pond and a pair of shady oaks. It was a nice place to sit and think, and it wasn't far away from the farm.

Danielle and Redman hung around the pond for a long time. Danielle concentrated on a bunch of ants swarming over a piece of candy she'd dropped in the sand. Ants were lucky. They didn't have any problems. They never had to move.

"What is Mom *doing*, Reddy?" she asked the big paint. "It's so crowded over on the Coast. Ugh. And me with manure all over my boots. I'm sure I'll fit right in living at the beach. Little Miss Cow Pie, just like Dylan says." She sighed. "I guess we'll have to wait and see, won't we, boy? You and I will still be together, anyway. We'll find a place for you."

Redman nibbled grass and listened patiently, his eyes liquid and wide. Danielle wondered if he sensed the changes that were about to happen. She hoped not. She wouldn't want her horse to feel as miserable as she did right now.

On the way home, Danielle saw a horse van lumbering out of her driveway. Down in the lower pasture she saw horses, too. New ones: a mare and her baby colt.

They were actually here! Hopeful Farm horses in her own backyard! Danielle couldn't help feeling excited about that. Redman pricked up his ears, quivered his nostrils, and neighed.

From a distance, the colt looked more like a little deer than a horse. *He's so cute,* Danielle thought as she watched him move with quick, tense steps. Like his mama, the colt was wearing a halter with a lead line attached. At the other end of the lines, Alec Ramsay was leading the two horses around the pasture.

The longer she watched, the harder it was for Danielle to tell who was guiding whom. Most of the time they all were following the mare. Occasionally Alec led her baby away from her. Whenever the little colt decided to go his own way, Alec didn't fight him. They looked like a family out for a rambling Sunday-afternoon walk.

Danielle rode closer. Alec spotted her and waved, gesturing for her to come ahead. She rode over to the gate, dismounted, and walked through. *What does he want?* she wondered.

Once inside the lower pasture, Redman whinnied and threw up his head. On the other side of the field, the mare danced around and moved beside her baby protectively. Danielle walked Redman ahead.

"Hey, can you give me a hand here?" Alec called to Danielle when she was within shouting distance.

Danielle cautiously led Redman forward. Alec smiled at her. His eyes were blue and sharp. He wore jeans, a flannel shirt, and sneakers.

"You're Danielle and Redman, right?" he said. "I'm Alec Ramsay. This is Prima and the little guy here doesn't have a real name yet. We're calling him Little Buddy for now."

Danielle nodded. "Hi," she said in a small voice, feeling a bit in awe of the handsome jockey.

"Listen, I'm going to try an experiment and turn Little Buddy loose." Alec pointed to the upper fence. "Can you ride up along the fence back there where you just were? When I let the colt off the lead, just keep an eye out in case he makes a run at the fence. If he does, try to flag him down. I don't think he'll go for it, though. Okay?"

"Sure," Danielle said shyly. What else was she

supposed to say? Alec Ramsay seemed friendly enough, even though right now she wished she'd never heard of him.

Prima nickered softly. She was a dark bay mare with darker legs, and a black mane and tail. Her chest was deep, her hocks and shoulders high. The colt's coat was a rich seal brown, even darker than his dam's, as dark as brown could be without being considered black. He had a fine, delicate head, long spindly legs, and straight knees. His eyes were large and fired with excitement.

"Pretty colt," Danielle said. "Is he the Black's?"

Alec nodded proudly. "Uh-huh."

That made sense, Danielle thought. "No wonder he's so dark," she said. "Do you think his coat will stay that way?"

"He'll change some," Alec said. "They all do. Coloring usually favors the dam's line more than the sire's. I don't imagine he'll lighten up too much, though. He's already four months old."

Danielle smiled at the colt and then did as Alec had asked. When she and Redman were in position, Alec let the colt off his lead. After standing stock-still for a second or two, the colt plunged away, swerving off with quick little steps. He flung his hind legs high in the air and spun around, then zigzagged off, going his own way. He was definitely enjoying his first taste of freedom.

Prima stood beside Alec, watching her baby frolic. For the next few minutes, no one else seemed to move. All eyes were on the colt as he dashed around the pasture. Despite her mixed feelings about Alec, Danielle found herself mesmerized by the beautiful little colt, just like Alec and Prima. He was a magnificent sight to behold.

Alec let Little Buddy run on his own a while longer. Finally, he managed to catch the colt by the halter and clip on the lead line. He waved thanks, and Danielle rode back to the barn. When she looked over her shoulder, she saw Alec, Prima, and Little Buddy continuing their tour of the pasture. The three of them stayed out there for a long time. They didn't return to the paddock until she was through washing and grooming Redman.

Danielle glanced over at Alec, feeling her mood darkening again. In a way, she almost wished Alec Ramsay was more of a jerk. How could she hate someone who seemed so nice and was so loving and kind to his horses?

She watched Alec and the horses for a moment longer from outside the fence, then walked up to the house. Her mother was waiting for her inside the front door, looking preoccupied. Danielle knew what *that* usually meant.

Trouble.

CHAPTER FOUR

No Way Out

"Nice colt, that Little Buddy," said Mrs. Conners as she stepped out onto the porch and leaned against the railing. She and Danielle both looked over to the paddock, where Alec was washing Prima. The mare was playing in the spray, enjoying her bath. When it was Little Buddy's turn, the colt tossed his head and gave a plaintive whinny at the first splash of water.

Danielle's mom took a deep breath. Her face was weary-looking and tight. "Listen, Danielle," she said quietly. "There's something else we have to talk about."

Danielle frowned. A sinking feeling swept over her, as if she already knew what her mother was about to say. Somehow she must have known it all along, and yet...

"I think you realize that Redman can't come with us when we move."

Danielle's brain refused to register the words. She wouldn't let it. It had to be a joke, a mistake. Her ears were playing tricks on her.

"I spoke with a man this morning, a Mr. Sweet. He has a big farm over in Albritton. He's agreed to buy Redman. I think he said he has a daughter a little older than you."

Danielle just stared at her mother, her eyes wide, still not believing what she was hearing. "But *why?* Why can't we bring Redman?" she finally managed to say. "He's part of the family, too."

"We're going to have enough to worry about, getting ourselves settled in a new place, without dragging some poor old horse along with us," Mrs. Conners said. "I'm sorry, Danielle."

"But why do we have to leave Wishing Wells?" Danielle wailed. "Let's just stay here."

"We simply don't have a choice right now, hon. Times are too hard." Mrs. Conners reached out and smoothed back a strand of hair that had fallen across Danielle's forehead. "Listen, I just heard from your dad. Let's give him a call. He wants to talk to you."

Danielle's mother walked into the kitchen and punched the numbers into the telephone. Then she silently handed the receiver to Danielle and left the room.

This isn't happening, Danielle told herself. *There*

must be some way out of this mess. She'd thought up some pretty good schemes before. Maybe she could come up with something now. She had to. And fast.

Her dad answered the phone. At the sound of his voice, Danielle almost started to cry. "Dad?"

"Danielle? Honey, is that you?" Mr. Conners said. Then Danielle heard him yell at someone to be quiet so he could hear.

"Hi, Dad. Yeah, it's me."

"Danny! How are you?"

"Okay," Danielle said slowly, even though it wasn't true at all. "Where are you? You sound so far away."

"I'm in Alabama, sweetheart."

At first Danielle's dad didn't say much except how much he loved her and missed her. She missed him, too. It made her feel sad hearing his voice, as mad as she was about everything else. In the background she could hear someone plunking on a piano.

When her dad finally got on the subject of the move, he told it to her straight. "You're a big girl, Danielle," he said. "You can handle it. You're going to have to. That's all there is to it. We have to do what's best for the family."

"But what about Uncle Al? He's lent us money before. Couldn't he…" Danielle began.

"Al can't help this time, sweetheart. He's in

worse financial shape than we are right now."

"But even if we do move, we just *can't* sell Redman," Danielle pleaded. "Julie Burke said maybe we could get a stall for him at Overton. They have so many barns over there, and half the stalls are empty."

"Julie's dad doesn't own Overton, Danielle. He only works there," Mr. Conners said patiently. "Besides, you know it's not fair to ask Julie or Jimmy Burke to take on Redman. That means buying his feed and being responsible for him."

"Yeah, but..." Danielle began.

"And you'll probably be living a couple hundred miles away."

"Couldn't we take him with us?" Danielle asked again. *"Please?"*

Her dad must have heard the desperation in her voice. His tone softened. "Honey, I know this is hard for you. But think of Redman a second, okay? I hear that this Mr. Sweet has a big ranch with plenty of roomy pastures for Redman to play in. The old guy will be happy there. And I'm sure Mr. Sweet will let you come visit Redman if you ask."

Danielle knew everything her father was saying was true. But that wasn't making her feel any better. It was making her feel worse. "Sure, Dad," she said with a sigh.

"And your grandma isn't going anywhere," Mr. Conners went on. "You can pay her and Redman a visit on your next vacation. And I bet you can even stay in Wishing Wells all summer."

Danielle didn't answer. Now she could hear men's voices laughing and talking in the background on the other end of the line.

"Wait a minute, Danny," her dad said. The noise behind him was getting louder. "Honey, I have to go. I have a set starting soon. Tell your mother I'll call back later. Love you."

"Love you, too," Danielle said miserably.

She hung up the phone and walked out to the porch. Collapsing onto the wicker couch, she thought about all the things her dad had said.

Vacations, Danielle thought, staring up at the branches of the big oak in their front yard. *Right.* As if Mr. Sweet's daughter was going to say, "Hey, there, stranger, come on over and ride my horse any time you want."

She got up and went to look for Dylan. She found her brother in the toolshed, as usual. This time he was disassembling an old carpet sweeper.

"Dad says we have to sell Redman," Danielle told him. "Can you believe it?"

Dylan didn't glance up from his screwdriver. "Well, what did you think was going to happen? Yeah, I can see it now. Maybe we can take Redman with us and we'll all live in a tent on the beach together."

"Don't be stupid, Dylan," Danielle said sharply.

Her brother finally stopped what he was doing and looked at her.

"What are you whining about, Danielle?" Dylan said impatiently. He waved at the rusty box stapler, the broken sewing machines, and other assorted pieces of junk around the toolshed. It had taken him years to find all of those treasures and drag them home. "Do you think I'm going to be able to keep any of this stuff?" He threw down his screwdriver, and for a second Danielle thought her brother might jump up and break something.

Then, just as quickly, Dylan was back to being Mr. Cool again, his eyes shining softly between narrow lids. "Forget it, D. The Coast will be great. You can be a beach babe. I'll be a surfer dude."

"Yeah," Danielle said, biting back tears again. "That'll be great."

CHAPTER FIVE

Saying Good-bye

Over the next week, Danielle's mom seemed to be on the phone practically every minute, making arrangements for the move. Dylan spent most of his time sulking in the toolshed. When his friends came by, he started giving away his scavenged trophies. They left with armloads of gears or springs, an old blender, or machine parts. No one went away empty-handed.

Alec Ramsay moved into the cottage beside the stable. Beyond a brief good morning or good night, barely a dozen words a day passed between Danielle and the young stranger living in the Coop. That was fine with Danielle. He probably sensed how she and Dylan were feeling and kept his distance.

Once, during Alec's first few days at the farm, Danielle did ask him about the Black. When Alec talked about his horse, she noticed that his eyes seemed to smile. Danielle's mom spent more time with Alec. She said he was the most grown-up-acting eighteen-year-old she had ever met. He'd been to the Middle East and Europe and other faraway places, she said, and sometimes he seemed so mysterious it was almost scary. Danielle didn't care about Alec at all. She was still so angry about losing Redman that she wished he would just go back to wherever he came from and stay there. *Why did he have to come here with his fancy, high-priced horses?* she asked herself about twenty times a day. *Why can't he just leave us alone?*

Since the Black and some other Hopeful Farm horses were being stabled at South Wind, only a few miles away from the Conners farm, Alec was over there much of the time. He offered to take Danielle for a visit one afternoon, but she excused herself, telling him she'd already made plans to go riding with Redman and Julie. Turning down a chance to meet a horse like the Black was something she would never have imagined herself doing. On the other hand, she could never have guessed his owner would be kicking her out of her own house, either.

As busy as Alec was with the horses at South Wind, he hadn't forgotten about Prima and Little Buddy. Bill Spicer had already started working full-time for Alec, and one or the other of them was usually around the barn. Together they had fixed up a desk, chairs, and filing cabinet for an office on one side of the tack room.

With the new horses and vets, trainers, and other horse people coming and going, the farm was becoming a very busy place. Little Buddy seemed to grow every day. It all should have been very exciting, Danielle thought. Somehow, it wasn't.

The late-fall weather turned damp and cold. Some nights the temperature dropped close to freezing. All the horses were given stable blankets to help keep them warm, and extra rations of feed. Little Buddy refused his blanket, preferring to cuddle up close to his mama, letting the closeness and warmth of her big body protect him from the chilly night air. Alec may have been used to the brutal winters in upstate New York, but Danielle could tell the weather surprised him. A lot of people thought Florida was sunny and warm all the time.

With everything that was going on, Danielle's regular after-school rides with Julie soon were history. Her friend was very understanding. After their last ride, Julie had come back to the Conners farm, where she met Billy and the new horses. Danielle could tell Julie was a little disappointed, though. She really wanted to meet the famous Alec Ramsay.

The days came and went. And the time for Redman's departure came relentlessly closer. Danielle tried not to think about it too much. When she did, she focused on remembering what her dad had said, how she should think about Redman instead of herself. *Sure,* she told herself, *think how much happier Redman will be living on a nice big spread in Albritton than being stuck in some rundown stable on the Coast.* That would be the best she could possibly afford. She thought of Redman spending his days romping around wide green fields, chasing butterflies and cloud shadows. Wouldn't it be better for him in a place like that?

And then it arrived: D-Day. The day Mr. Sweet had said he was coming to pick up Redman and take him away.

School went by in a blur. Luckily, Danielle managed to get through the ordeal without being called on by any of her teachers. Not that it mattered. Homework didn't seem terribly important right now.

Being around Julie, her best friend, almost made matters worse. All she seemed interested in was Alec Ramsay and the Black, even though she knew how Danielle felt about them. "Have you seen the Black yet?" Julie asked Danielle as they sat together on the bus coming home from school that afternoon.

"No," Danielle said, shrugging. At this moment, the Black was about the last thing on her mind.

"I'm sure you'll get to see him," Julie said excitedly. "I mean," she added, catching herself, "before, um, you guys…"

"Leave," Danielle finished for her. She stared out the bus window.

Julie looked sympathetic. "Sorry."

"That's okay." Danielle sighed. "You know that Mr. Sweet is coming over this afternoon to pick Redman up, don't you?"

Her friend nodded slowly. "I feel so bad for you, Danielle. I can't imagine what I'd do if Calamity was going away somewhere."

"I keep wondering about Mr. Sweet's daughter and what she's like. She's never even met Redman, and he's going to be *her* horse. I have no idea if she'll take good care of him. Why does she want a horse she's never seen?"

Julie shook her head. "I don't know. But I'm sure Redman will be okay. Anyone who knows horses can see he's a great horse." She turned around and frowned at some fourth-grade boys two seats behind them who were starting to argue noisily.

Suddenly, Danielle had an idea. "Wait a minute," she said, grabbing her friend's arm. "You have a cousin who lives in Albritton, don't you? Isn't his name Kenny or something?"

"Freddy," Julie corrected.

"Could you ask him if he knows Carol Sweet?"

"Why don't you just call her up and talk to her yourself?" Julie asked.

Danielle drew back against the window. "I couldn't do that."

"Why not?"

"What if she's mean or something?"

Julie laughed and gave Danielle a playful punch on the arm. "You're crazy, Danielle. I'm sure she's really nice. But okay, if you really want me to, I'll try to find out what I can."

"Thanks, pal. Want to come home with me? I could use some company today."

Julie thought a moment. "Well, I'm supposed to help my mom with some chores, but if Redman's leaving, I'm sure she'll understand."

The bus dropped Danielle and Julie off at Shootzy's Diner, their regular stop. The place wasn't much: just a lunch counter, some tables, and a grill. They went inside so Julie could call her mom. After Mrs. Burke had given the okay for Julie to go to Danielle's, the girls picked up their bikes from the back of the diner and pedaled for the Conners farm as fast as they could.

Redman wasn't in his pasture when they got home. Danielle's heart began to pound. Could Mr. Sweet have taken him away already? Julie put a hand on Danielle's arm. "Take it easy, Danielle," she said reassuringly. "He's around somewhere."

Danielle ran to the barn and almost cried with relief when she found her horse in his stall, munching hay. Stepping inside, she threw her arms around the big paint's long neck and pressed her head hard against his forehead.

"Are you okay?" Julie asked, leaning against the stall door.

"I'm all right," Danielle replied, her voice muffled. "Redman's the one I'm thinking about. I'm so worried he'll think we don't love him anymore."

"Redman knows you love him," Julie assured her, coming over to stroke Redman's neck.

"But he's lived with us all his life." Danielle's voice broke. "I feel like we're betraying him."

Redman pricked his ears and whinnied, probably wondering why he was being penned up in the barn when it was time for a ride.

"Everything will be okay, pal," Danielle whispered.

All too soon, she heard the sound of a heavy vehicle coming up the driveway. "They're here," Julie said. Danielle went to the door and saw a big blue horse van stop outside the stable. Two men got out. The older one in the sports jacket had to be Mr. Sweet, Danielle figured. He walked straight to the front door of the house. The younger guy in the baseball cap started sliding a wooden gangplank up under the door of the van.

Danielle stepped into the barn and returned to Redman's stall. She turned her back to Julie and pressed her face flat against Redman's neck.

"Come on, Danielle," Julie said. "Crying's not going to help."

Danielle swept a hand across her eyes. "Sure," she said, her voice muffled by the lump in her throat.

A few minutes later, Mr. Sweet came into the barn with Danielle's mom. He was a handsome, wealthy-looking man with gray hair and deeply suntanned skin. His tailored navy jacket had the initials CWS monogrammed on the front. He was talking with Danielle's mom about the Coast and how much he liked it there.

"We have a cottage near Stewart, you know," Mr. Sweet was saying. "Lovely place. Do you and your husband play golf? Nothing like a round of golf by the sea to invigorate the soul." Behind his back, Julie rolled her eyes at Danielle.

"Hello, ladies," Mr. Sweet said. He nodded politely to Danielle and Julie when Mrs. Conners introduced them, but after that he treated them both as if they were invisible. Danielle moved out of the way as Mr. Sweet walked straight to Redman's stall. The paint gave a little jump when Mr. Sweet led him outside. For a second, Danielle thought he might even rear up on his hind legs.

"Whoa," Mr. Sweet called, and Redman stopped obediently. Danielle walked over to her horse. The big paint lowered his head, his mane falling down over his eyes. With a sigh, she pushed the mane back and rubbed his forehead tenderly.

Danielle looked up at Mr. Sweet. "You'll take good care of him?"

Mr. Sweet nodded. "Of course, young lady. My kids will be good to him."

Kids? Danielle thought. *Isn't he buying Redman for his daughter?* She moved her hand from Redman's forehead to his mane, then walked slowly past her horse one last time, trailing her fingers along his red coat. Redman turned his head and whistled to Danielle as he was led to the truck.

Danielle wanted to call after him, but the words froze in her throat. *He's* my *horse,* she told herself. *How could he belong to anybody else?* How could she live without him? Sobbing, she ran blindly toward the tack room.

Julie started after her, but Mrs. Conners touched her on the arm and shook her head. "Let's leave Danielle alone for a little while," she said.

Inside the tack room, Danielle tried not to hear the sound of Redman's hoofs on the gangplank as he was loaded into the van. Grief and hot anger rushed through her. She couldn't believe this was actually happening. Then came the rumble of the van's motor and the grinding of gears.

Redman was gone. Who knew when she'd ever see her beloved horse again?

And there was nothing she could do about it.

CHAPTER SIX

More Surprises

Days passed with hardly a word on Redman from his new owner. All Danielle knew was that her horse had arrived safely at the Sweet ranch. Her mother was doing a million things, making arrangements and setting up job interviews. Danielle moped around in her room, avoiding Alec and his horses as much as possible. The whole situation was so depressing that she had a rough time just getting up in the morning.

None of the kids Danielle asked at school knew anything about Carol Sweet over in Albritton. Julie hadn't been able to get in touch with her cousin yet. But it had been almost a whole week now. Danielle couldn't wait any longer.

When she and Julie got off the school bus at Shootzy's on Friday afternoon, Danielle asked her friend to try calling Freddy again.

"Okay," Julie said. "If you want me to."

Danielle knew her friend was shy about bothering her cousin. He was in high school and probably didn't appreciate his little cousin's bugging him with silly phone calls.

No one was inside Shootzy's except the plump, round-faced woman who owned the place. "Hey, Mrs. Perez," Danielle and Julie called in singsong unison.

"*Hola, jovenes.*" Mrs. Perez returned their greeting with a smile. "*Coma estas hoy?*"

"*Muy bien, gracias,*" Julie said, practicing her Spanish. Danielle bought Cokes at the counter and the two of them headed to the pay phone in the back of the diner.

Danielle dug a quarter out of her knapsack and gave it to Julie. She watched anxiously as her friend picked up the receiver and dropped the coin in the slot. Julie punched in the number and waited as the phone on the other end of the line started ringing. Danielle put her head close to Julie's so she could hear the conversation.

"Hello?" a voice grumbled sleepily.

"Hi, Freddy. It's me, Julie."

"Julie?"

"Your cousin. How are you doing?"

Freddy sneezed. "I have a cold, if you're really interested."

"I'm sorry. But listen, I was wondering if you had

your last year's high school yearbook around? A friend of mine needs some information on someone."

"What am I, a private eye?"

Julie rolled her eyes at Danielle.

"Please, Freddy."

"Right." Freddy said, sneezing again. "Hold on," he said impatiently. Danielle could hear drawers opening and closing; then Julie's cousin came back on the line. "What's the name?"

"Carol Sweet."

"Okay," Freddy said. "Let's see if I can find the index of this stupid thing. Wait a second… Here it is," he said finally. "Carol Ann Sweet. She's a year behind me."

"What does she look like?" Julie asked. She listened and turned back to Danielle.

"She looks like a girl," Freddy said.

"That's it?" Danielle mouthed to Julie.

"That's it?" Julie repeated into the receiver, shooing Danielle away. She listened to her cousin a moment longer, then said, "Thanks for the help, Freddy. We really appreciate it." She turned to Danielle. "He says she's a blonde. Then he asked me if there was anything else he could do for me, like my homework or maybe copy the dictionary over the weekend." Julie chuckled. "Freddy can be a real jerk when he wants to."

"Sorry, Jule," Danielle apologized. "I didn't mean to stir things up between you two."

"No big deal," Julie said. "But it looks like we're back to square one. What next, Fearless Leader?"

Danielle took a deep breath. "We'll just have to call Carol Sweet, I guess," She got the number for the Sweet ranch from Information and dropped another quarter into the coin slot. "Here goes."

A girl answered the phone. "Sweet residence."

"Hello. My name is Danielle Conners," Danielle said in her best grown-up telephone voice. "I'm calling for Carol Sweet."

"This is she."

Danielle tried to keep the desperation she was feeling out of her voice. "Uh, hi. You don't know me, but I'm the person who used to own the horse your dad bought for you last week. I, uh, was just sort of wondering how he's doing....How has he been making out over at your place?"

"Who?" Carol Sweet asked.

"Redman. My—I mean, your—new horse."

"New horse?" The older girl sounded truly puzzled. "I've had the same horse for three years. Her name is Mimosa. She's a four-year-old Arabian mare."

Now it was Danielle's turn to be confused. "But didn't you..."

"Oh, wait a minute," Carol said. "I know! You're

talking about one of those horses that Daddy just bought. He's shipping them out tomorrow, I think." Her voice was off-handed and vague. Danielle heard a beep on Carol's phone line, signaling another incoming call.

"Wait...Shipping them out?...Tomorrow?...Where to?" Danielle asked frantically.

"North Carolina, I think. It's a riding camp up in the Smoky Mountains that Daddy owns. His new partners need stock. You know, gentle, easygoing horses for beginners."

Mr. Sweet's daughter had to be wrong. He wouldn't send Redman away! Hadn't he promised to take good care of him?

Julie looked at Danielle questioningly. Danielle shook her head and held up one hand, silently telling her friend to wait.

"You mean he isn't staying at your farm?" Danielle asked.

The incoming call beeped again. "Not that I know of," the older girl said. "Wait a second, let me pick this up."

The phone line clicked and went silent as Danielle was put on hold. Her legs began to feel wobbly, and she leaned against the wall. She stared blankly at the phone, her mind swimming.

The line remained silent for a few more

moments. Suddenly, there was another click, and a dial tone rang in Danielle's ear.

"I can't believe it!" Danielle cried. "She cut me off! What a creep."

Her hand trembled as she hung up the receiver. Taking a deep breath, she told Julie what Carol had said.

Julie snapped her fingers. "So he wasn't talking about his daughter after all when he told you his kids would be good to Redman. He meant the kids at his riding camp."

Danielle clenched her fists in anger. She could just see poor Redman now, suffering through never-ending days of circling a corral or practicing stops and starts with a pack of little monsters taking turns on his back. It wasn't fair.

Being a riding-camp horse might be okay for other horses, but definitely not for Redman. He needed wide-open fields and trail rides. He couldn't be stuck in a training ring all day. He just couldn't.

No way.

♔ CHAPTER SEVEN ♕

Letting Go

Danielle looked around the empty cafe, feeling betrayed. She just couldn't believe what Carol Sweet had told her. Julie couldn't believe it, either. "North Carolina!" she gasped. "That's so far away."

"So *this* is my reward for training an easygoing, bridle-wise horse," said Danielle. "He gets shipped off to Kiddie Land."

Julie nodded. "If he was a hot head like Calamity, the riding-camp people probably wouldn't have wanted him."

Danielle winced.

Behind the counter, Mrs. Perez was humming a tune as she washed some glasses in the sink.

"What am I going to do?" Danielle said, slumping down on a stool with her Coke. She wasn't feeling very thirsty anymore.

Julie put a hand on Danielle's shoulder.

"Nothing," she answered. "There's nothing you can do."

Danielle threw her hands up in the air. "There must be *something*."

"Try to look on the bright side," offered Julie. "It might not be so bad for Redman up there in the mountains."

By now Danielle was about to reach her boiling point. She'd never been so furious in all her life. It must have shown in her face, because Julie quickly tried to change the subject.

"Hey, are you coming to Viv's birthday party?" Julie asked. "Tonight's Friday night, remember?"

Danielle shook her hair down in front of her eyes. "I don't care about Viv's stupid party. And I don't care about the stupid mountains or the stupid beach." She kicked the counter in frustration every time she said the word stupid.

Mrs. Perez suddenly stopped humming. She looked at the girls in the mirror over the sink and frowned.

Julie took Danielle by the arm. "Come on," she said, pulling her outside and into the sunlight.

Danielle jerked her arm away. "Don't drag me around like that," she snapped.

"Quit acting like a hysterical brat," Julie told her.

"Leave me alone," Danielle said, kicking at the dirt. How could Julie be thinking about a party at a time like this? And who wouldn't be hysterical? She'd been tricked, lied to, and betrayed.

"You're overreacting," Julie said. "I'm just trying to keep you out of trouble."

Danielle took a few deep breaths, but the angry flashing light in front of her eyes was still there. Then, slowly, it began to fade. Julie was right. *I am being a brat,* Danielle thought. And how could she get so angry with her best friend? She had to get ahold of herself.

"I'm sorry," Danielle told Julie. "You're right."

"Hey, like I said before, I'd probably feel the same way if I were losing Calamity," Julie said.

Danielle nodded. "Let's not talk about it for a while, okay?"

"It's a deal," said Julie, and the two of them went to get their bikes.

By the time Danielle reached home, her anger had turned to despair and then to anger again, back and forth a hundred times. When she told her mom the riding-camp story, Mrs. Conners was surprised to hear that Redman was being shipped up North. She hugged her daughter sympathetically. "I really am sorry, honey," she said. "I had no idea."

Danielle sulked through dinner and then headed straight to her room, dragging her feet heavily down the hall. A little while later, her mom knocked on the door. "Can we talk?" she asked.

Danielle rolled over on her bed. "I guess so," she said, her voice muffled.

"You're taking all of this way too seriously, Danielle," Mrs. Conners said. "A horse isn't a pet. You're big enough to know that. Remember last year when your dad sold Buster? You didn't see him carrying on about it."

"But Redman is part of the family," Danielle said, sniffling.

"He also weighs almost a thousand pounds," her mother pointed out.

Neither of them spoke for a moment. Finally, Mrs. Conners sighed. "I know how you must feel, Danielle," she said. "But you have to learn to let go."

"Couldn't we just drive over to Sweet's ranch so I could see Redman one last time before he leaves?" Danielle pleaded.

Her mother shook her head firmly. "It's almost time for bed, dear, and I still have a hundred things I have to get done by tomorrow. Even if I could take you, Danielle, why drag out your good-byes? It only hurts more."

She sat down on the bed and patted Danielle's knee. Danielle hugged her mom, who kept patting, not saying anything.

After a while, Mrs. Conners got up and left the room. "I'm here if you need me, honey," she said, closing the door. Danielle flopped back on her bed, feeling very alone again. She flipped through magazines and tried to listen to music, but she ended up just staring at the walls, thinking.

Getting a ride from her mom wasn't the only way to get to Albritton. Maybe there was another way...

Around nine, Julie called from Viv's party.

"Any cute boys there?" Danielle asked.

"Just the usual crew. We miss you, you know. Everyone's been asking about you."

"Thanks," Danielle said. "Listen, Julie, I'm sorry about this afternoon. I really was acting like a jerk."

"Well, you sound better now. Too much better. What happened?" Julie asked suspiciously.

"Nothing, really. I just talked things over with Mom. I'm going to try 'letting go,' like she suggested."

"Well, you certainly were letting go this afternoon. I thought you were going to kick *me* for a second there."

Danielle laughed in spite of herself. "I feel really stupid now about all that. I'm going to have to apologize to Mrs. Perez when I see her."

Julie's voice sounded suspicious again. "I get the feeling you're not telling me something."

Danielle hedged. "We can talk about it later."

Now Julie was really curious. "Danielle, I *know* you."

"Quit being so nosy, Julie."

"C'mon, Danielle, *please*. We're best friends. If you can't tell me…"

Danielle hesitated. "Okay, I'll tell you, but you can't tell *anybody* else. Promise?"

"Promise." Danielle heard a door close.

"I'm in the bathroom now," said Julie, giggling. "So what's up?"

"Well, you know that bus schedule they have by the cash register at Shootzy's? I was looking at it the other day. There's a night bus to Albritton at three-fifteen A.M. and one coming back at six. The ticket costs only four dollars each way. With luck I can find the Sweet ranch, see Redman, and get home again before my mom ever finds out."

"Are you crazy?" gasped Julie. "You can't do that!"

"I know it sounds nuts." Danielle's voice trembled slightly. "But of all the people in the world, you're the one person I thought might understand."

"I do, but…"

"Well, I can't really let go of Redman unless I see him one last time. All I want is to share a couple of Pop-Tarts with him and watch the sun come up together like we used to."

"What if your mom finds out?" Julie asked.

"I know it'll be risky. But I have to say good-bye!"

"I still think you're crazy."

"Maybe."

Julie didn't say anything for a minute. "I guess you're going to do what you're going to do," she said slowly. "But be careful, okay?"

"I will," Danielle promised.

That night, after setting her alarm for 2:45 A.M., Danielle tried to get some sleep, but it was hopeless. She lay awake in bed, feeling nervous. Her room was so quiet she could almost hear the beating of her own heart.

At close to three o'clock, Danielle slipped out of the house. A full moon brightened the sky, and the air was cold and damp. She was wearing both a sweater and a denim jacket, the same clothes she'd worn the day before. She'd slept in them to make sure she was ready to go when the time came. Her knapsack was slung over her shoulder. In it were twelve dollars and seventy-five cents, a box of raspberry Pop-Tarts, a bag of carrots, and some peppermint candy for breakfast with Redman.

Back in her room, on her pillow, Danielle had left a note for her mother, just in case she didn't make it home on time. She quietly wheeled her bike away from the house. Then she uneasily began pedaling up the driveway and out to the empty road. As she turned onto the pavement she hit a pothole and almost fell over.

What am I doing? she asked herself. *Julie's right. I*

am *crazy*. It was the middle of the night. She was alone. She felt scared. She'd never done anything like this before. She took a deep breath, letting the cold air deep into her lungs. *I'm going to see Redman*, she told herself, *that's what I'm doing*. She tightened her grip on the handlebars and she pressed down harder on the pedals.

She rode to Shootzy's and parked her bike behind the diner. Then she walked over to the bus stop, which was a lone bench outside the diner's front door. It was completely dark except for the streetlight shining over the parking lot and the brightness of the winter moon.

Standing under Shootzy's awning, Danielle watched the long, dark road for signs of life. She glanced at her watch, worrying that somehow she might have missed the only night bus. Headlights appeared in the distance. A car passed. Then another. A truck. She looked at her watch and listened to her heart race, feeling anything but brave.

Finally, the bus came, right on time. Danielle moved under the streetlight to flag it down. When the bus door opened, she stepped inside.

"Round trip to Albritton, please," she said, handing the driver the fare.

The burly man eyed Danielle critically. She was tall for her age but she was still only twelve. And it was after three in the morning on a Friday night.

"Isn't it a little late to be out here alone, young lady?" the driver asked.

"It's an emergency, sir," Danielle explained. "I have to see my dad. He's working as a security guard at that new all-night shopping center."

The driver raised one eyebrow and gave Danielle another up-and-down glance. Now she wished she'd spent a little more time thinking up a believable story. Then, after what seemed like forever, he shrugged, took the money, and handed Danielle her ticket. She walked quickly down the aisle, past a few snoring passengers, and found a seat.

With a groan, the bus rumbled onto the county road. Danielle settled back in her seat and gave a sigh of relief as the bus picked up speed.

She was on her way.

❦ CHAPTER EIGHT ❧

Sylvie

Danielle stared blearily through the dark window of the bus and sighed. The trip seemed to be taking forever, and what exactly was she going to do when she got off the bus in Albritton? All at once she felt very frightened and alone.

She thought back to the afternoon when Mr. Sweet had taken Redman away, the trusting look in her horse's eyes as she turned him over to his new owner. Waves of sadness washed over her and tears dribbled down her cheeks. A long, low sob that she couldn't choke back rose up from deep inside her.

"Going far?" said a scratchy voice.

Danielle dabbed her eyes with the back of her hand and turned away from the window. She saw a face in the cone of light shining down from the overhead reading lamp in the seat across the aisle. It belonged to a woman about her mom's age. She was wearing a floppy gray felt cowboy hat and a tropical-print shirt.

Danielle flushed in the darkness and nervously tried to collect herself. Did she really want to talk to this person? The woman didn't look very threatening, but Danielle wasn't in the habit of giving out personal information to strangers. She broke her eyes away from the woman's gaze. "Just up the road."

The woman began to dig around in her purse. She pulled out an orange, peeled it, and looked over at Danielle again hopefully. "Care for a wedge?"

Danielle shook her head. "No. Uh...no thanks."

"Go on, darling. Take it."

Danielle cocked her head and glanced at the woman. Plainly she was just trying to be friendly and didn't mean her any harm, not on a bus with other passengers anyway. And oranges were naturally sealed.

"Well, okay, sure," Danielle stammered, shrugging.

"There's nothing like a nice orange to cut through the nasty smell inside these old buses," drawled the woman.

Danielle accepted the orange wedge and paper napkin the woman offered. She took a bite of orange and quickly wiped her eyes with the napkin.

"Here. Take another," said the woman, passing

Danielle a few more napkins. "These juice oranges can get mighty sticky."

"Thanks." Danielle wrinkled her nose. "What is the bad smell in here, anyway?"

"Diesel fumes. Dirty socks." The woman smiled. "It's probably better not to ask."

Danielle smiled back, feeling herself begin to relax a bit.

"You're lucky, kid. I've been on this beast all the way from Atlanta." The woman extended her hand to Danielle. "My name is Sylvie. What's yours?"

Danielle shook the woman's hand. "I'm Danielle," she said.

Sylvie leaned over the armrest of her seat and looked up the aisle at the passengers in the front of the bus. "These long trips aren't so bad," she said. "You know what I like to do? Watch people and try to guess where they're going. Maybe they're on a business trip, or going home to see their folks, or meeting someone for a secret romance. Or maybe they're running away from home."

Danielle wondered if that was what Sylvie was thinking about her. Probably. The thought suddenly gave Danielle something new to worry about. Would her new friend turn her in to the bus driver?

"Like that guy in the Dolphins cap sitting in the front seat behind the driver," Sylvie went on. Danielle gave a sigh of relief. "Did you see him when you got on? I figure he's a long-haul truck driver heading to pick up a rig in Miami. Or maybe he's a big-time jewel thief in disguise who's on the run from the cops."

Danielle tried to smile. "Well," she said politely, "everyone's going someplace, that's for sure."

"The fun part is wondering why." Sylvie's gaze flitted around the bus. She looked back at Danielle conspiratorially. "It's all just pretend, but it's fun." Danielle rubbed the corners of her eyes with the napkin again. "Are you feeling better, kid?"

Danielle nodded slightly.

"Want to talk about it?" Sylvie asked. "Are you having trouble at home?"

Danielle shook her head. "Nothing like that."

Sylvie kept talking, about her favorite movies and TV shows. She mentioned her pet cat, and when she asked if Danielle had any pets, Danielle hesitated. Then she opened up and spilled Redman's whole story to this woman she'd met only a few minutes before.

As she listened, Sylvie nodded encouragingly. She knitted her eyebrows together when Danielle finished. There was nothing disapproving or judgmental in her voice when she spoke again.

"Well, Danielle, you're a regular education. I've heard some strange yarns in my time, but a breakfast date with a horse? Now *that's* a good one."

"Well, it's true," Danielle said, feeling a little stupid.

Sylvie chuckled and pointed to the little golden horseshoe pin stuck to Danielle's denim jacket. "I'm sure it is. I can see you're a horse person. Don't worry, honey. It'll all turn out."

"I hope so," Danielle said. "Redman always trusted me. I feel responsible for him."

"Like I said, everything will be all right." Sylvie said. "You'll see."

Yeah, Danielle thought, *for me, maybe*. But what about Redman? She wasn't so sure that things would work out for her horse. "How can you be so sure of that?" she asked Sylvie.

"It's the same for everybody, love. People get swept up by things they can't control. Trying to stop them is like standing in front of a steamroller. If you don't get out of the way, all you do is get yourself run over."

Danielle nodded slowly. That was *exactly* how she felt.

Sylvie reached out and touched her arm. "Sometimes you might feel like you're all alone in this world. But you're not."

"I always had Redman," Danielle said.

"And you always will," Sylvie told her. "He'll always be in your heart."

"But I don't think I can live without my horse,"

Danielle said. "Redman's the only one who..."

Sylvie sat up straighter in her seat. "Listen, Danielle. I've been from one end of this country to the other dozens of times, and I've met all sorts of people. If there is one thing I've learned, it's this: When things start getting tough, you have to be cool-headed. Things change. You'll see. Just don't panic. Stay calm."

A few minutes later, the bus pulled into Albritton. Danielle stood up as the driver announced the stop. She turned to her new friend, feeling a little sad at having to say good-bye. Here was someone she would probably never see again, someone she hardly knew. But for some reason she felt very close to Sylvie.

"Thanks for the orange," Danielle said. "And all the advice."

"Might get cold out there tonight. Rain maybe. Better button up."

Danielle smiled and zipped her jacket. "Okay. I'll be careful."

The woman's gaze swept over Danielle again and fixed on the little gold horseshoe pin on her jacket. "Hey, you're wearing your horseshoe upside down. The open end should always be at the top. Didn't you know that? Otherwise all your good luck will fall out."

"Really?"

Sylvie grinned. "Try it and see."

Danielle readjusted the pin on her jacket, right side up. She needed all the luck she could get right now. Sylvie smiled and gave her a thumbs-up sign.

Danielle mumbled an awkward good-bye, shouldered her knapsack, and stepped off the bus.

Pennies from Heaven

Danielle waved to the bus as it rumbled off into the night. She thought she saw Sylvie waving back to her from one of the windows. Or maybe it was just a reflection in the glass.

The one-room Albritton bus depot was closed for the night. A young soldier was dozing on a bench beside the front door. Danielle gazed down the empty streets and then up at the night sky. Clouds were beginning to hide the stars of the Big Dipper to the north. She turned her collar up against the wind, touching the pin on her chest for luck.

The streetlights cast a dull glow over the sidewalk. Danielle reached in her back pocket and pulled out the map she'd copied from the phone book before she left home. If she had figured everything correctly, the Sweets' ranch couldn't be more than a couple miles away.

Well, this is it, Danielle thought. She forced to

the back of her mind the growing fear that made her want to turn around and go home. It would all be worth it if she could see Redman just one more time. At least she could try to make him understand. Taking a deep breath, she set off to find her horse.

At nearly four in the morning, the streets were empty of all but a handful of cars. A few panel trucks were making their early-morning deliveries. The sidewalk along Main Street led past storefronts draped in shadows. Danielle clenched her jaw and concentrated on putting one foot down in front of the other. The fear was continuing to build inside her. If only she had someone to talk to! And what if she got caught? What would her mother say if she knew she was here? Danielle forced herself to focus on just one thing: Redman.

The wind freshened suddenly, cold and damp and gusting from the north. Drops of rain sprinkled Danielle's face and shoulders. Then more drops came splattering everywhere.

Oh no, Danielle groaned to herself. The rain fell harder, and she broke into a run, heading for the nearest refuge, a strip mall about a hundred yards away.

The wind blew in sweeping gusts as the pelting raindrops exploded in tiny fountains under the streetlamps. Quickly Danielle's clothes were drenched.

Finally reaching shelter beneath an awning, she wiped her face, then shook herself like a dog in a vain attempt to get dry. Outside, the rain came in ever stronger waves, hammering the aluminum awning and draining off it in sheets. Low black clouds were sweeping over Albritton as fast as the wind and rain.

The only thing to do was wait, Danielle decided. Setting out in the rain would be stupid. Maybe the storm would blow over quickly.

A police car sped by, and Danielle drew back into the shadows. Her heart pounded inside her chest. *This is crazy,* she told herself. *And dangerous.* She glanced around. She had to find someplace to hide until the rain slacked off. The strip mall was much too exposed. There were streetlights in the parking lot and more lights in front of the stores. It would look to anyone passing by as if she was loitering around a strip mall in the middle of the night. Not a very smart idea.

She walked quickly past the storefronts, looking for a spot to hole up in for a while. At the other end of the mall, in front of the Goodwill Store, she found the perfect hiding place.

It was a Goodwill box, where people could leave their donated clothes when the store was closed. It was about the size of a small car and shaped something like a street-corner mailbox. The hatch was just wide enough for Danielle to scrape through. She climbed up, opened the hatch, and tumbled headfirst into a pile of musty old clothes.

The faint odor of mothballs tinged the warm stuffy air. Danielle's heart was beating loudly, and she could feel its heavy thumping every time she took a breath. She removed her knapsack from her shoulder and fumbled inside it until she found her penlight.

With a flick of the switch, a quarter-sized spot of yellow light shone on mounds of pants, shirts, jackets, dresses, and shoes piled beneath and around her. Some of the clothing was folded neatly and packed in plastic bags. Others pieces were strewn in tangled heaps. It reminded her of the closet in her brother's bedroom.

As Danielle tried to make herself comfortable, she felt a lump inside the jacket she was using for a pillow. She reached into one of the pockets. The lump felt like a thick roll of paper or... She quickly pulled it out of the pocket and gasped.

Money!

The wad of bills had to be an inch and a half thick. Tens on top, with twenties underneath.

Danielle spread the cash in front of her and slowly counted out the bills, one at a time. *There's almost six hundred bucks here!* she thought.

She pinched herself to make sure it wasn't a dream. This was *real*.

She rubbed the notes together and stared at the faces on the bills as if they were pictures of long-lost relatives.

She'd hit the jackpot!

CHAPTER TEN

Sneaking Around

Danielle still couldn't believe it. Here she was, huddled inside a Goodwill box, holding more money in her hands than she'd ever seen in her life. Six hundred dollars, lying right there, just waiting for her to pick up.

She ran her thumb over the wad of cash again. An idea was taking shape in her mind.

This money could be the answer to all her problems. It was more than enough to buy Redman back from Mr. Sweet. He'd paid only five hundred dollars for her horse.

I have to find a way to keep Redman, Danielle told herself, *or at least find someplace in Wishing Wells where he can stay.* Anything was better than having him shipped off to some riding camp up north, where she'd never get to see him again.

Danielle fanned the bills. *Whose money was this?* she wondered. Had they missed it yet? It had to have been a mistake. No one tossed cash into a Goodwill box.

A car with a loud muffler rumbled through the parking lot outside. Danielle immediately shrank back into the pile of clothes, as if anyone could see her inside the metal container. A tug-of-war was starting up inside her head. *Should I keep the money or not?* she asked herself. *Why do I feel like a thief?*

That six hundred dollars belongs to somebody, a voice inside her head answered. *Taking it would be wrong.*

But maybe the person is so rich they won't care, Danielle argued back. *Is it my problem if somebody can't keep track of their own money?* She needed it. Redman needed it. If the person who'd thrown away all that cash didn't know what to do with it, *she* knew somewhere it could do plenty of good. It would be almost like giving to charity. Kind of.

She felt around inside the jacket again to see if there was a name tag or anything that might identify the owner. All she found was a label from some fancy store in New York. The voice inside her head said, *Just leave the money there. Maybe the real owner will call Goodwill and claim it.*

Then another voice countered, *Hello? Excuse me? Say no to the first break that's come my way in ages? I don't think so.*

Somehow I was meant to find this money, Danielle decided. *It wasn't just an accident or a case of finders keepers. The money was put here for me to find because Redman and I need it. A lot. And someday I'll pay the Goodwill people back. I'll just be borrowing the money for Redman.*

Carefully pocketing the cash in her wet jeans, she squeezed herself slowly through the narrow opening again, feetfirst this time.

It was still raining hard. Danielle looked around for a phone booth and found one in front of a store in the middle of the strip mall. Slipping through the shadows, she reached the phone, picked up the receiver, and punched in the number for Information.

"What city, please?" said the operator.

"Albritton. Do you have a number for an all-night taxi service?"

"One moment, please."

There were a few seconds of silence. Danielle glanced at her watch. It was four twenty-five in the morning. She was surprised she didn't feel more tired than she did. But the thought of seeing Redman again made her so excited that sleep was about the last thing on her mind.

From here on, everything will be okay, she told herself. She was on a mission. She pictured herself wearing camouflage military fatigues like a commando raider in one of those action movies Dylan was always renting from the video store. Here she was calling headquarters to get her coded instructions. She touched the wad of bills in her pocket. Its bulk felt reassuring. It also brought her thoughts back to earth. *Quit fooling around,* the voice inside her head said. *This is not a game.*

The operator gave Danielle the number of a taxi service and even dialed it for her. The taxi dispatcher who answered said they would send someone right over.

Danielle hung up the phone. She kept thinking about what Sylvie had said on the bus, about things working out if you just didn't panic. Things were changing, all right. And fast. Now she was a thief. She took a few deep breaths. *Don't panic,* she reminded herself.

The taxi took about ten minutes to arrive. It was an old station wagon with ROYAL LIMO SERVICE painted on the side. Danielle pulled her baseball cap down low over her face as she emerged from the phone booth and got in. She gave the stubble-faced driver the address of the Sweet ranch and slouched back in her seat.

Rain beat hard against the dark, tightly shut windows. The heater was blasting, and it was hot and stuffy in the car. Danielle's wet sneakers made her think wishfully of the rubber rain boots at home in her closet.

"Some weather we're having tonight," the driver commented idly, his voice rising above the slap of the windshield wipers and the noise of the motor.

Danielle didn't answer.

The driver glanced into the rearview mirror. "Pretty late to be out window-shopping, isn't it, miss?"

Danielle mumbled a sleepy-sounding "I guess so."

"Looks like you got caught outside in the rain. I have a towel in the trunk. If you want, I could…"

"That's okay," Danielle said, a bit clearer this time. "I'll be all right."

The driver shrugged, and from then on they rode in silence. Danielle touched her horseshoe pin and gazed out at the dark streets.

Soon the rain drumming on the roof began to soften. Danielle rolled down the window on her side. They were driving through a neighborhood of ritzy estates, each set on several acres of land.

"You're going to have to help me here, miss," the driver said. "I'm not too familiar with the streets in this neighborhood."

"Uh, sure," Danielle said. "It should be right up here, I think."

"You *think*?" the driver asked, sounding surprised. He gave Danielle a quick glance over his shoulder. "Don't you know? Isn't it a bit late to go visiting people when you don't know where they live?"

I really blew it this time, Danielle thought. "It's my uncle's place," she said quickly. "I'm from up North and I just got in on the bus. They're expecting me. Don't worry."

"The bus, huh? Traveling a little light, aren't you?" the driver asked suspiciously. "Where's your luggage?"

Danielle thought fast. "I'm only staying the weekend."

"I see," the driver said, though he plainly didn't believe her.

Danielle tried to stay cool, but nervousness was tying her stomach in knots. *Remember,* she told herself, *every minute you're getting closer to Redman. Stay calm.*

"Looks like the rain's letting up," the driver said, switching off the windshield wipers.

It was true. With a last rush of wind, the rainstorm stopped almost as quickly as it had started. The taxi driver began peering at street numbers and pulled off the road beside a mailbox set at the foot of a long, tree-lined driveway. The mailbox said SWEET.

"This will be fine," Danielle said, paying her fare with a ten-dollar bill from the wad in her pocket.

The driver's eyes nearly popped out of his head when he saw the roll of bills in Danielle's hand. She quickly shoved the wad back into her pocket.

"You sure they're expecting you?" the driver asked.

Danielle tried to sound tough. "Hey, what is this? Twenty questions? I'm paying the fare, right?"

The driver chuckled. "I suppose so, miss. Sorry."

"That's right," Danielle said firmly, and stepped out of the cab. "Keep the change," she said, closing the door behind her.

"Wow, two whole shiny quarters," the driver said sarcastically. "Gee, thanks!" With a clank, he put the cab in gear and drove off, grumbling about stingy rich kids.

Rich kid, Danielle thought. *Right.*

She put the taxi driver out of her mind and started up the driveway to the Sweet house. It was a huge place with tall white columns. The wide raised front porch was half the size of Danielle's entire house.

There was a long, low building just beyond the house. Danielle guessed it must be the barn. Now she felt like a spy on a rescue mission in some stupid movie. Walking on her tiptoes, she headed straight for the barn, wishing she could make herself invisible. What if someone looked out a window and saw her? *Don't think,* she told herself. *Just keep moving.*

Suddenly, a dog barked from the direction of the house.

Danielle froze.

Dogs. She hadn't thought of that possibility. Her breath caught inside her chest. Again the dog barked. She waited and watched, but no lights snapped on inside the house.

All at once, another thought crossed her mind. Maybe the dog wasn't in the house at all. Maybe it was outside. That would be even worse. She listened for another minute, wondering if the dog or anyone else might be wandering around the property this late. A night watchman, maybe, or a gardener who couldn't sleep.

Danielle fixed her attention on the barn door. There was no turning back now. Redman was in there. She ducked between some fence rails and walked quickly and quietly across the paddock.

Slipping into the dimly lit barn, Danielle breathed in the horsy odors she loved, familiar and comforting even in this strange place. Everything was clean and in its proper place, freshly painted and new-looking. A few horses were snoring in their stalls. She walked down the long corridor of mostly empty box stalls, peering into each of them anxiously. But there was no sign of her horse.

What if Redman isn't here? Danielle thought suddenly, beginning to panic. What if Mr. Sweet had already sent him away? *No,* she told herself firmly. Carol Sweet had said the horses weren't being shipped off to the riding camp until tomorrow. But what if she had been wrong?

Danielle paused outside the tack room. On the wall were pictures of a pretty blond teenage girl riding a beautiful Arabian mare. It had to be Carol Sweet and Mimosa, Danielle thought. In one photo, the girl was sitting on her horse, wearing a Western outfit and hat, and holding a blue ribbon. In another she wore a formal man's suit and was riding English-style, all straight back and perfect form.

Danielle gazed up at the row of yellow, red, and blue ribbons lining the wall below a shelf of trophy bowls and plaques. *Wow,* she thought. It looked as if Carol Sweet spent half her life taking riding lessons and the other half competing in horse shows. Danielle couldn't help feeling a little jealous.

She thought back to their phone conversation, trying to match the voice with the girl in the pictures. Carol had sounded a lot like she looked in the pictures, a stuck-up rich kid who always got everything her own way. A Florida princess. She probably had her daddy totally wrapped around her little finger, Danielle thought, sneering up at the photos. *Too bad* I *don't,* she added to herself. *Then I wouldn't be in this mess to begin with.*

Continuing to tiptoe down the aisle, Danielle

moved from stall to stall in search of her horse. In one box was an old Arabian mare with a white blaze on her forehead. Mimosa's dam, Danielle supposed. The mare was standing beneath a small overhead bulb, looking fat and tired, her head drooping. Probably sleeping, Danielle thought. She felt kind of sorry for her.

"Hello, old mare," she whispered. There was only the slightest twitch of the mare's long ears in reply.

A sudden rustling sound from the far end of the corridor made Danielle wonder if there might be a stable hand or groom somewhere in the barn. It was one more possibility she'd overlooked, one more thing to worry about. But she couldn't just stand here too scared to move for the rest of the night. Danielle swallowed. *Oh, Reddy,* she thought, *where are you?*

Creeping the rest of the way down the corridor, she peeked over the half doors, searching for her horse. Finally, she found him.

"Redman!" Danielle called softly. "Reddy, it's me."

The big paint responded immediately to her voice, greeting Danielle with a long, drawn-out whinny. She opened the stall door. "Shh," she said as she quietly slipped inside. "Act nice now, big guy."

Redman flicked his ears and started nickering.

Danielle hushed him, speaking quietly with her hands in a special language that only the two of them knew.

Danielle put her arms tenderly around her horse's neck. She had no idea how long she stayed there, just hugging Redman. It seemed like a very long time. *Okay,* she told herself finally. *Time to get out of here.* But first she had to write Mr. Sweet a note explaining everything.

Pulling a pen and a piece of paper from her bag, she began,

> *Dear Mr. Sweet,*
> *I'm sorry that*

Danielle groaned and crossed the line out. *No.* She wasn't going to start out apologizing. Redman was *her* horse, after all. And Mr. Sweet had lied to her.

What can I say that will make sense? Danielle asked herself. She tried to imagine the reaction Mr. Sweet and his snobby daughter would have the next morning when they came out and found Redman gone. Then she wondered what her own parents would do when they learned what had happened. It was better not to think about that right now.

Danielle started the note again. And again. Each time her words sounded more and more ridiculous, and she ended up crossing them out. How could she explain what she was doing? She wasn't even so sure herself.

The note she finally settled on was short and to the point.

> *Dear Mr. Sweet,*
> *I'm afraid there's been a mistake. My horse*
> *is not for sale and I'm taking him home. Enclosed*
> *is the five hundred dollars you paid for him plus*
> *seventy-five more to cover the cost of shipping*
> *him to your place in the van. I hope this doesn't*
> *inconvenience you too much.*
>
> > *Yours truly,*
> > *Danielle Conners*

She signed her name in large capital letters, then folded another piece of paper around the note to make an envelope. She addressed it to Mr. Sweet and put all the money inside.

Suddenly, she froze. What was that sound? One of the horses moving around in his stall? Or footsteps? Her heart began to race again. She was getting really jumpy now. Maybe her ears were playing tricks on her.

Taking a deep breath, Danielle carefully poked her head over the half doors and looked both ways up the corridor. All clear. She opened the door and led Redman forward. "Easy, boy, easy," she chanted softly.

They walked up the corridor together, past all the pictures, trophies, and ribbons. Danielle took her envelope, marked it PRIVATE, and taped it on the tack-room door. She was a little nervous about leaving a letter with so much cash in it like that, but under the circumstances it was the best she could do.

The big paint's nostrils swelled as he stepped outside. The night wind fanned his mane and tail. Danielle walked beside him, keeping her hands on his neck. *This is it,* she thought. *If we can just get away from here now without being seen....*

Redman snorted.

"Shh. Easy, big guy, easy," she repeated.

Danielle led her horse over to the paddock fence and stopped. Using the bottom rail, she boosted herself up and let her weight come down on Redman's back. Redman shifted beneath her, and she clucked quietly in his ear.

Danielle hadn't ridden Redman bareback in ages. But now, she didn't have much choice. She didn't want to steal a saddle or other tack from Mr. Sweet. Besides, all this sneaking around was getting to her. She felt enough like a thief already, even after leaving the money.

But Redman is mine, she reminded herself. *He'll never belong to anyone else.*

She looked back over her shoulder at the barn and the Sweets' house. Thankfully, there was no sign that anyone was coming after them.

Danielle gave the paint a pat on the neck. "We did it, boy!" she said. "We did it!"

A moment later, Redman swept Danielle off into the cold, dark night.

CHAPTER ELEVEN

The Long Way Home

To Danielle, the clip-clop of Redman's hooves sounded like loud gunshots as they made their getaway down the driveway. When they turned onto the main road, Redman broke into a gallop. Danielle let him run all he wanted. She was happy to put as much distance as possible between herself and the Sweet ranch.

After about a mile of splashing through mud puddles, Danielle tried to get her horse to ease up. They had a long way to go, and she wanted Redman to save his strength. "Slow, Redman. Slow now. We're just going to take it easy, okay?" Her hands pleaded with his neck, and the paint began to change gaits, slackening his pace. "That's it, boy. We don't need to hurry. Slow, slow."

Now that she had some more time to think, questions began whizzing around inside Danielle's mind. What would Alec Ramsay say when she showed up with Redman? Somehow she figured that, if anyone might understand how she felt about her horse, it would be Alec. But Mom and Dad and Dylan?...

And what about the more immediate problem of how she was ever going to get home by sunup? It would have been a tricky enough job taking the bus home alone as she'd originally planned. Now she had to make it on horseback.

They edged off the side of the road and started through an open field. Danielle figured she could get most of the way home by keeping to the backcountry. Taking shortcuts would be quicker, too.

Unless she got lost.

The truth was, she'd never been trail riding as far as Albritton. She knew she had a good sense of direction, though. With luck, she could find her way home from here, even in the dark. Wishing Wells couldn't be much more than twelve miles away. Danielle rubbed Redman's neck. At least the two of them were together again. As a team, they could get through anything.

Redman trotted steadily along. Soon they turned off on a trail that led through fenced-in rangeland for cattle and sheep. About a mile later, Redman suddenly shied at a gnarly tree stump beside the trail. Danielle let him sniff it to convince himself that it was nothing to fear.

"It won't hurt you," Danielle said reassuringly. "Don't worry."

They walked on through an orange grove and more pastures. Redman kept acting skittish from time to time, and Danielle had to kid him along, pet him, talk to him—anything to coax him ahead. It would be light before too long, and there was still a long way to go.

Though the moon broke through the clouds only in brief glimpses, Danielle tried to use it as a compass to keep them pointed in the right direction. Her attention remained focused on the dips and bumps in the trail directly in front of her horse's hooves. But she was tired now and finding it difficult to concentrate.

Why did she feel so ashamed all of a sudden about taking that money from inside the jacket? And where was she going? Home to face the music? Away from here, that was about all she knew. Danielle reached to touch her pin for luck.

It wasn't there!

Her lucky horseshoe pin was gone.

Frantically, she felt all over her jacket, but found nothing. She checked her pockets. Empty. Pulling Redman to a stop, Danielle turned to look behind her. Where had she lost the pin? It could be anywhere.

Her heart sank. She wasn't superstitious, but it

certainly had been a wonderful coincidence she'd found the money in the Goodwill box just after turning the pin right side up. If finding that money wasn't good luck, what was?

Well, it's too late now, Danielle thought. *The pin is gone.* And she wasn't about to go back and look for it in the dark, either. She braced herself and urged Redman on with her legs.

Soon the wind seemed to blow cooler, and the moon became completely hidden by clouds. Danielle shivered and prayed it wouldn't start raining again.

A bird cried in the night, and other sharp, scary animal noises sounded from somewhere not very far away. Suddenly, Redman began making a series of little jumps. Danielle grabbed the paint's neck to keep herself from falling off. She could feel his trembling muscles beneath her arms.

A moment later, the sky opened again. Rain fell in big, splashing drops, soaking every fold of Danielle's already damp clothes. Redman struggled on through the mud, past trees bent with the weight of drenched leaves.

Danielle leaned forward, feeling tired and beaten. Redman's closeness was all that kept her going. The big paint's breathing comforted her. Being on her own out here in the night would have been a lot more terrifying.

Redman thrashed his head against the rain as Danielle kept coaxing him forward. "Come on, boy," she told him. "I'm getting just as wet as you are. Come on, Redman. Let's get home. Fast."

Toward daybreak the rain stopped. Danielle glanced at her watch. Though it seemed like forever, not even an hour had passed since they'd left Sweet's ranch. The wind switched again and slacked off. The clouds blew away. Stars came out for a brief moment before dawn, swimming through the sky before Danielle's sleepy eyes.

She almost cried aloud with relief. At last the long night was over. Redman seemed to perk up a bit, too, his ears standing up on his head like the blades of open scissors.

The sense of relief didn't last long, however. Time was running out. Back home, her mom would be getting up pretty soon. Then she would find the note Danielle had left on the bed in her room. Danielle didn't even want to guess how her mom was going to react to *that.*

The thought made her urge Redman on faster. Yet after a mile she slowed him up again. *What's the point in rushing?* she asked herself. *There's no way we're going to be home in time.*

She gave Redman a pat on the neck. "Getting hungry, fella?" she said. "It's time for a break. Let's eat."

They stopped by the side of the trail and shared the last of the soggy Pop-Tarts Danielle had brought for breakfast. This little adventure was certainly turning out a lot differently from the one she'd imagined when she'd started out. Danielle leaned close and clung to Redman to keep warm. They watched the sunrise for a few minutes and then started off on the road again.

As they rode, Danielle daydreamed about a nice hot bowl of oatmeal. She gazed up into the heavens. Only the eastern sky seemed to have any color to it: pastel swirls of blue and pink. A flock of white birds flapped by. It was the kind of morning that could make you feel as if the world was all fresh and full of possibilities. At least it could if you weren't soaked to the bone and worried about twenty different things at once.

Well, Danielle told herself, *at least I still have Redman.* That made up for a lot.

"What's going to become of us, big guy?" Danielle asked. She stroked and patted her horse's neck. "How am I ever going to explain to Mom where I got that money? I just wish I had a little more time to think. I know we can work something out, if only…"

Redman bobbed his head sleepily. Around them, the rangeland was coming alive with animals out foraging after the rain: squirrels, rabbits, blue jays, and doves. Up ahead, Danielle could see great blue herons standing around a puddle in the trail. From a distance, the giant birds looked like old men gathered together to chat. As Danielle drew nearer, she could pick out their long necks and stilt-like legs. They stalked from their bath as she and Redman came up, glaring at her with angry eyes, as if she was breaking up their party.

The sun began to rise higher, and Danielle felt its delicious warmth seep into her. Mom and Dylan were awake by now for sure. She wished she could call to let them know she was okay, but the back trails and fields she was crossing were far from any phones. Maybe that was just as well. She was really scared now of what her mom might say.

Danielle sighed. Maybe she shouldn't go home at all. Taking that money—and Redman—had been a really stupid move.

Her mom was going to kill her.

The Black

Danielle rode Redman through seemingly endless groves and rangeland. She needed a place to rest and think things out. After a while she began recognizing landmarks from her trail rides with Julie. She followed one familiar-looking trail through a stand of live oaks and came to a place where the two of them had camped out last summer. Perfect. It was just what she was looking for.

Gator Grotto was a natural spring, like a small swimming pool at the bottom of grassy hollow, in a field miles from the nearest road. It was named for a large rock at the water's edge that looked like a half-submerged alligator. Years ago, on her first visit here, Dylan had played a prank on her, pretending the rock was a real alligator and giving Danielle the scare of her life. Her brother had thought it was the funniest joke in the world, laughing so hard he nearly choked. Danielle had wanted to break his neck. In truth, the nearest live alligator was about fifty miles away.

Danielle led Redman along the rim of the hollow. She gazed down to the pool at the bottom and the springwater bubbling up from the lime rock. This was a great place to swim and, she remembered, to feed the minnows with pieces of stale bread. Gator Grotto was owned by the state or the county or something, so you didn't have to worry about some shotgun-toting rancher wanting to chase you off his property.

At least there was plenty for Redman to drink, Danielle thought. That was the most important thing. The spring water had a mild sulfur smell, but as far as Danielle knew, it wouldn't kill you to drink it, especially where it was bubbling up directly out of the rocks.

Redman whinnied for joy at the sight of the water and hurried down to the water's edge. As the paint lowered his head to drink, Danielle leaned over the pool to look at her reflection. Her blond hair was black with splatters of mud and grime. A gray shadow of dirt and sweat ringed her neck. "Ugh," she said.

She picked her way down to the path that ran alongside the spring. Lizards skittered around the edges of the pool, searching for insects. Just for fun, Danielle caught one and then let it go.

Danielle had swum here with Dylan a few times before. It would be okay to take a quick dip, she decided. A moment later she jumped into the water, clothes and all. The water was cold and refreshing. One piece at a time, she pulled off her clothes and stripped to her underwear.

After finishing her bath, Danielle cleaned her mud-spattered jeans and jacket as best she could, then spread them on rocks to dry in the sun. Exhausted, she stretched out in the sun herself, too tired to think.

She fell into a restless sleep and awoke to feel something spidery touching her face. She screamed and sat up quickly, but it was only Redman. He was standing over her and puffing breaths of warm air at her face. "Reddy!" she scolded him. "You scared me half to death."

The sun was nearly straight overhead by now. Danielle rubbed the back of her neck and looked at her watch. It was a little before eleven. Yikes! She jumped to her feet and ran down to the spring to throw some cold water on her face. Her clothes were almost dry, but her hair was still matted and wet.

She had just finished putting her clothes back on when Redman lifted his head from where he was munching grass and whinnied, giving her another fright. Hoofbeats. It sounded like a bunch of horses were trotting toward her along the trail leading to the grotto. The hoofbeats drew closer and slowed down.

Danielle quickly climbed up to the rim of the hollow to see who was coming. Reaching the top, she caught her breath. Julie, Dylan, and Alec Ramsay were riding up the trail, less than fifty yards away!

At first, Danielle was thrilled to see familiar faces. Then she realized what their arrival meant. They were looking for *her!* She and Redman were doomed.

The three riders came closer. Alec was riding astride a magnificent black stallion, a horse with a coat the color of the thickest, darkest velvet imaginable. Danielle knew immediately that the horse was the Black.

The stallion was beautiful, incomparable to any other horse she'd ever seen. It wasn't just his size or his perfectly proportioned muscles. It was something else, even more than his regal bearing. Something magical.

Dylan pointed toward her, and Danielle waved meekly.

"We figured you might be out here," Julie called. "You know how long we've been looking for you? All morning. Your mother is going crazy. And Mr. Sweet is about to call the cops."

"What do you think you're doing?" Dylan said as

he rode up. "And where did you get all that money?"

"I guess Mom heard from Mr. Sweet, huh?" Danielle said.

"He called first thing this morning," Julie said, "before your mom even knew you were gone."

Alec nodded. "She talked him out of calling the police for the moment, but I'd say you have some explaining to do, Danielle."

Saddle leather creaked as the three riders dismounted. "You look like a wet rat," Dylan said. Danielle scowled at her brother, though it was probably true. She could feel her hair sticking to her forehead and hanging around her face in damp, flattened strings.

She turned from all the accusing words and faces and stared into the water, looking at Redman's reflection in the pool. A few moments later, the other horses came down to join the paint at the water's edge. The Black and Redman were checking each other out, sniffing the air for signs of fear or aggression, but the two of them seemed content to accept the spring as neutral territory.

Danielle gazed at the Black in awe. Now she realized why so many people made such a big deal about him. *He's truly the most spectacular horse I've ever seen,* she thought.

Alec squatted down, watching her, obviously waiting for her to give some sort of explanation.

When Danielle didn't say anything, he stood up. "Okay, then. Let's get moving, everybody."

But Dylan wasn't about to let her get off so easily. "You sure are something, Danielle. Do you really think anything is going to change? Where do you think Redman is headed now? Right back to Mr. Sweet. And *you're* probably going to jail."

Danielle spun around and stuck her chin out. "No way. I paid…"

"Leaving money and a note isn't a legal deal. What you did is called horse stealing. Nothing's changed, Danielle. I repeat, nothing. Unless the two of you plan on camping out at Gator Grotto for the rest of your life. And where'd you get that money anyway? Did you rob a gas station or what?"

"I found it."

Dylan snorted. "Sure."

"That's enough, you two," Alec said impatiently. "Stop arguing. We have to reach a phone and call your mom before the police really do get involved."

Danielle felt anger boiling up inside her. She tightened her lips, then jumped on her brother, dragging him to the ground. They tussled and rolled around until Alec broke it up.

"I *did* find it," Danielle said. She blurted out the whole story, telling Alec, Dylan, and Julie about the bus, the rain, finding the money in the Goodwill box, and the ride from Mr. Sweet's.

"Redman and I were coming home," Danielle finished. "Really, we were. We just needed some time to rest."

She turned to Julie, her best friend, looking for sympathy.

"Come on, Danielle," Julie said. "You can't win. You're just making things hard on everybody, including yourself."

Danielle blinked. *Some friend you are,* she thought. "But I gave Mr. Sweet all his money back," she insisted, "and more."

"Oh, that's brilliant," Dylan sneered. "Did you ever think that maybe that wasn't your money to give away? I mean, you didn't just find it blowing down the sidewalk. That money belongs to Goodwill, not you. Taking it wasn't right."

"I don't care what you say," Danielle argued. "It wasn't just some coincidence. I was meant to find that money."

Dylan started to laugh, looking at Alec for approval. He didn't get it.

Alec turned to Danielle. "Life's funny like that sometimes," he said. His voice was sympathetic and gentle. "Things seem to happen for a reason. But that doesn't mean…"

"Tell me about it," snapped Danielle, in no mood for pity.

"I will," Alec said.

Great, Danielle thought. *As if a famous guy like Alec Ramsay could ever understand.* He was treating her like some confused little kid. Why had she ever thought he might be any different from the others?

"I had the Black taken away from me once," Alec continued.

"Really?" Danielle said, interested in spite of herself.

Alec nodded. "That's right. And the Black came back to me, even after his rightful owner reclaimed him."

"Yeah, but…"

"Good comes out of bad all the time, Danielle. Look at me. If I hadn't been shipwrecked when I was a kid, I never would have met the Black."

Danielle heard Alec's words, but they barely registered in her brain. What possible good could come from sending Redman off to some riding camp up North? But she had to admit, Julie and Dylan and Alec were right. There was no way out for her and Redman. She felt cornered, frightened, and alone. Her whole body seemed to deflate, like a balloon with a leak in it.

"Come on, Danielle," Julie said softly. "Let's get to a phone before your mom has a complete fit."

Danielle must have looked so pathetic that even

Dylan softened up a bit. He shuffled his feet and put his hands in his front pockets. "Sorry, D. I didn't mean to be so hard on you."

Danielle tried to smile. "That's okay."

Dylan stepped beside her and put an arm around her shoulders. "You know we're all on your side."

Alec nodded. "Try to look at it like a kind of test, Danielle," he said. "A very smart man told me something once. He said that winners are the ones who can best handle their problems. That's some of the most useful advice I've ever heard."

Danielle stared at Alec with a blank expression. *Easy for you to say when you have a horse like the Black,* she thought.

"Winners?" she said weakly. "I don't care about winning. I just want to be with my horse."

"Guess I think in racing terms a lot," Alec said. "But you get the picture, right?"

"Yeah," Danielle said in a small voice.

Alec nodded in the direction of town. "Let's hit the road, shall we, guys?"

CHAPTER THIRTEEN

Good News

Stringing out in single file, the four horses and their riders started on the trail back to Wishing Wells. Alec and the Black led the way, with Danielle and Redman bringing up the rear, behind Julie on Calamity. In front of Julie, Dylan bumped and bounced his way along, riding a swayback Arabian mare.

"Who's that Dylan's riding?" Danielle asked.

"Gypsy," Julie said, falling back to ride beside Danielle as the trail widened. "She belongs to my Aunt Trix."

Danielle shook her head in disbelief. "And she lent her to Dylan?"

Julie grinned. "I told Aunt Trix it was an emergency."

"I can't believe you actually got him on a horse. He hasn't been riding since we were little kids."

Julie chuckled. "Look at him squirm. His backside must be killing him."

"No wonder he's so cranky," Danielle said.

"What was that?" Dylan called back over his shoulder.

"Nothing, Dylan," Julie said. "We're just admiring your form."

Dylan shifted in his saddle. "Having me come along was Mom's idea, not mine. Do you really think I care what happens to my sister and her stupid horse?"

Danielle knew Dylan didn't really mean it. He was probably just trying to cheer her up by acting the way he usually did. It was hopeless, but she appreciated the effort anyway.

Alec didn't seem to be paying much attention to any of them, Danielle noticed. Every once in a while he took a cell phone out of his jacket pocket and punched in some numbers, but the portable phone didn't seem to be working. "I dropped it this morning and must have broken it," Alec said. "I guess we'll just have to wait until we find a pay phone."

He put his cell phone away and concentrated on the trail ahead. Danielle imagined he was probably pretending to be some fearless Western sheriff leading his posse home after tracking down the archcriminal Danielle Conners.

But as Danielle watched Alec, she again began to

wonder what kind of guy he really was. Gossip magazines and TV shows were full of stories of teen celebrities who, because of their talent or whatever, spent so much time training or working that they never had a chance to just be kids. It was probably that way with Alec Ramsay.

Danielle sighed. Something inside her wanted to bolt with Redman. *Things seemed so hopeful for a while there,* she thought. Now everything looked pretty bleak. Dylan was right. Nothing had changed. Nothing, except that now she was up to her ears in trouble.

Out of habit she reached up to touch her lucky horseshoe pin for reassurance and felt the empty spot on her jacket. *Talk about bad luck,* she thought. Almost the moment she lost that lucky pin, everything had started going horribly wrong.

As the riders drew nearer to town, they came to a two-lane county road. One car passed by slowly, then another, giving the horses a wide berth.

They stopped at a gas station and found a phone so Danielle could call home. Julie and Dylan went inside to buy sodas and something to eat. Alec watered the Black and the other horses. The magnificent stallion watched Danielle, silent and knowing, like some fantastic Egyptian statue.

There's no way out now, Danielle thought. *Might as well get this over with.* Taking a deep breath, she bravely picked up the receiver. She'd never felt so anxious in all her life.

The phone rang only once, but it wasn't Danielle's mom who picked up on the other end. It was her dad! Just hearing his voice gave Danielle new hope. If anyone could turn this situation around, it was him. "Dad?!" she gasped. "What are you doing home?"

"Danny! Where are you? We've been so worried!"

Danielle swallowed. Oh, boy. She was really going to catch it now. If her mom had called her dad home all the way from Alabama, she was in real trouble.

"I'm okay, Dad. I'm with Dylan, Julie, and Alec. We're at a gas station just outside of town."

Her father's voice sounded both relieved and angry. "Get yourself home *now*, young lady," he said curtly. "You've scared your mother and me half to death. How on earth did you come up with such a crazy stunt? Do you realize how dangerous that was? And where did you get that money?"

"I didn't steal it," Danielle said in a small voice. "Honest."

"Well, you can tell us all about it when you get here."

"Okay, Dad. Sorry." She hung up the phone, hating the idea of having let him down. How she was ever going to be able to explain everything?

Dylan came out of the gas station and silently handed her a candy bar. She grabbed his arm. "Why didn't you tell me Dad was home?"

From the look on her brother's face she could see that he had no idea what she was talking about. "Dad's home?"

Danielle nodded. "That was him on the phone."

Dylan shrugged. "He must have flown in this morning after we left the house to look for you. Uh-oh. You're in trouble now, sis."

Julie tapped her on the shoulder. "Come on, Danielle," she said. "Let's go home."

Danielle kicked at the ground with her sneaker. "And where *is* home exactly?" she mumbled. "I don't know where it is anymore. I know where it *used* to be. We're moving to the Coast, remember?"

"Get over it, Danielle," Dylan said, sounding fed up. "You're acting like a loser, just like Alec said."

"That's not what I said at all, Dylan," Alec pointed out, coming up behind them. "What I meant was that winners know how to handle their setbacks."

"Well," Dylan said, "it's sort of what you said. And she *is* acting dumb."

Danielle looked at Alec accusingly. Mr. Winner, Mr. Good-Comes-from-Bad, was the same guy who was taking over her family's farm. Alec must have read her thoughts and known they were directed at him. Surely her face wasn't hiding how she felt.

A momentary look of hurt flashed over Alec's face. He held up his hands in mock surrender. "Hey, Danielle. Take it easy. I just answered an ad in the paper. I don't want to chase your family out of your home."

"Yeah, what are you blaming Alec for?" Dylan demanded. "Moving to the Coast is Mom and Dad's idea, not his."

Danielle blinked and looked at the ground. "I didn't say anything, Dylan."

"You didn't have to." Dylan said. Julie just looked at Danielle and shook her head. Danielle flushed, too angry and embarrassed to speak.

"I think we all could use a rest and a little lunch," Alec said. "I'm starved, and I bet the horses are, too. Come on, let's go."

Danielle mounted up with the others. Redman bobbed his head wearily, dragging himself ahead. The strain of the long, hard ride had taken its toll on the old boy. He shook his head as a pair of fat green-headed horseflies buzzed around his ears. Danielle swatted at them, shooing them away and brushing the back of Redman's head. She stroked his mane apologetically. "Just a little farther and we'll be home, boy. Don't worry."

Home, she thought. *Right.*

When they arrived at the farm, Mr. Conners was

standing on the porch in a black western-cut shirt and jeans, looking anxious. "Danny! Dylan!" he called when he spotted them.

Danielle and Dylan waved to their dad and then turned to Julie.

"I'll take care of Redman and Gypsy, you guys," Julie said. "Go ahead."

Danielle and her brother jumped down from their horses and ran to their dad. They hadn't seen each other in months. Danielle knew nothing she could have done mattered as much as the fact that she and her father missed each other terribly. Mr. Conners took her and Dylan in his arms and gave them both a big bear hug.

"I've missed you guys so much," Mr. Conners said.

Danielle stepped back and caught her breath. "We missed you too, Dad."

"Me, too," Dylan said.

Mr. Conners looked over to the paddock, where Julie and Alec were untacking the horses, and waved. Then he turned to Dylan. "Go help Julie with the horses, will you, son? Danielle and I have to talk."

"Sure, Dad," Dylan said, retreating quickly.

Arm in arm, Danielle and her dad walked inside to the kitchen, where Danielle's mom was waiting. Mrs. Conners gave her daughter a quick hug, then sighed and shook her head.

"You know how glad we are to see you're okay, Danielle," her mom began. "But..."

"I know you must be mad..." Danielle said.

Mrs. Conners crossed her arms. "*Mad?* Now why should you think that? Leaving me a note and taking off in the middle of the night! Just who do you think you are, young lady?"

"Wait a minute, Mom," Danielle said. "Let me explain." She poured out the whole story of the previous night's adventure and about finding the money in a Goodwill box.

Her dad glanced at her mom a moment, then turned to Danielle. "Well, that money is going straight back to Goodwill as soon as I can make the arrangements with Mr. Sweet."

"Yes, sir," Danielle said softly, hanging her head.

"And what was I supposed to think when I heard you left nearly six hundred dollars in Mr. Sweet's barn?" Danielle's mom said. "I was imagining...well, you don't even want to hear some of the things your brother was suggesting."

"I hope you know I wouldn't steal it."

Mrs. Conners took Danielle by the arm and stared straight into Danielle's face. "What do you call taking money that doesn't belong to you?"

"Listen, Danny," her dad said. "We know how you feel about your horse. But you *do* see now that taking that money was wrong, don't you?"

"Not to mention running off in the middle of the night, wandering around the streets of Albritton, and breaking into Mr. Sweet's barn?" her mom added. "And *stealing* a horse."

"But I didn't break into..." Danielle started to say.

"Danielle..." warned her dad.

Danielle swallowed her pride and looked down at her muddy sneakers. "Yes, Mom. Yes, Dad."

"You're grounded, Danielle. Big time," her mom said firmly. "Now, go get yourself cleaned up. I have to talk with your father some more about all of this." Danielle nodded and hurried upstairs.

After taking a shower, Danielle came back into the kitchen. She took a soda from the refrigerator and looked out the window over the sink. Alec and her dad and mom were talking out on the porch. The three of them looked very serious. Danielle didn't want to know what they were talking about. Julie and Dylan were nowhere in sight. Danielle guessed that they must have taken Gypsy home.

When Alec left, Danielle's mother called her outside.

Mr. Conners motioned to one of the old rocking chairs. "Sit down, honey. Your mom and I want to speak with you."

Here it comes again, Danielle thought. She was never going to hear the end of this whole episode.

Mr. Conners cleared his throat. His voice sounded soft but serious. "For one thing, Danielle, you should know that the actual reason I came home wasn't because of anything you did. The truth of the matter is that a gig the band and I were scheduled to play was canceled, so last night I bought a ticket home as a surprise to you and Dylan and your mom. I had no idea about any of this horse business until I arrived here this morning."

"I was wondering how you got here so fast," Danielle said.

"Well, I would have canceled the gig anyway when I heard what you were up to."

"Oh." Danielle lowered her head. "Sorry."

Her dad held up his hand. "We're just glad you're safe, Danny. But there's something else. We just had a little talk with your friend Alec Ramsay…"

My friend? Danielle thought. *Right.*

"His main interest here is in the land, the use of the barn, and pastures for his horses. We've been talking things over, and he's agreed to a temporary lease deal instead of buying us out, lock, stock, and barrel."

"What does that mean?" Danielle asked.

"It means that Alec and I will arrange to make the bank payments on the farm together. He'll be using the Coop as his headquarters. Since he plans on traveling a lot, to races and other horse farms, he thinks the Coop will suit his needs just fine while he's here. So, for the time being, the family will stay on in the big house. It'll give us some breathing room while we sort things out."

Danielle wasn't sure she understood. "You mean we're not going to be moving to the Coast?"

"No," her mother said quickly, "that's *not* what your father is saying at all. We still plan to move, just not right away. Pretty soon we'll get everything lined up on the Coast, and then we'll go. But for now, this deal with Alec is too good to pass up." She looked at her husband. "I suppose Mrs. Mack won't be too happy about this, but I think we can handle her."

Danielle was stunned, flabbergasted, then over-joyed. "That's great!"

"And..." Mrs. Conners paused and smiled proudly at her husband. "Tell her, Kyle."

Mr. Conners's blue eyes lit up. "Oh, it's nothing to get too excited about. Just that one of my songs is climbing the charts in Australia."

Danielle grinned. "Really?"

"Yep. I might even get a tour over there. If noth-ing else, the extra royalty checks should keep the bank off our backs awhile."

Danielle looked back at her mom. She was the one who had been so hot for them to move in the first place. Why had she changed her mind so quickly?

Mrs. Conners read the expression on her daughter's face and shook her head. "I've sent out a few résumés. The job market is a little softer than I thought over on the Coast. Maybe it'll get better soon. We'll see. In the meantime I'll keep working on my Web page designs. I'm already getting more work. And with this new song of your dad's..."

Danielle jumped up and hugged her mom tightly. Then she blurted out the question that had been forming in her mind ever since she'd heard about her parents' change in plans. "So Redman can stay?" Danielle asked hopefully. Her parents exchanged glances. "At least until we're certain we're going to move?" Danielle's voice trailed away. This was hardly a time to be asking for favors, but she didn't have much of a choice.

Mr. Conners looked down at his daughter. "You'll have to talk with Mr. Sweet about that. *After* you apologize to him for all the trouble you caused. It's entirely up to him."

"But it's okay with you?"

"We all love Redman, too. You know that. But a deal is a deal. He belongs to Mr. Sweet right now. And you have to remember that we're still going to move to the Coast eventually." He glanced again at Danielle's mom, who gave a slight nod, "But as long as we *are* here, I suppose Redman can stay, too. If Alec doesn't mind, of course," he added.

Danielle started jumping around as if she was on a pogo stick. Even with all the "buts" and "ifs," this was better than she had dared hope.

"You'd better talk it over with Mr. Sweet before you get too excited, Danielle," cautioned her mom. "Technically, he owns Redman. He might not want to sell him back."

"He will. I *know* he will. He just has to."

"I wouldn't push him too far, Danielle." Mrs. Conners said. "We're pretty lucky he's been nice enough to hold off calling the police as it is. And your father already promised we would bring Redman over to his place as soon as you came home."

"Just let me try, Mom. Please." Danielle rushed over to the phone. Then she dialed Mr. Sweet's number and held her breath.

☙ CHAPTER FOURTEEN ❧

Unexpected Allies

Danielle listened anxiously as the Sweets' phone rang. She knew she had to apologize for all the trouble she'd caused him. But she was determined to change his mind about keeping Redman.

A man's voice answered the phone. "Sweet here."

"Hello? Mr. Sweet? Um...Hi. This is Danielle Conners. You know, Redman's owner? I mean," she corrected herself quickly, "I *used* to be his owner." She reminded herself to sound humble and apologetic.

"Well, well, well. If it isn't our little runaway."

"Runaway?..." Danielle held out the receiver and stared at it, shocked. "I didn't...I'm not..."

"I know very well who you are, miss. Now, could you please inform me of the whereabouts of my stock and give me one good reason why I shouldn't call the police in on this affair?" His voice sounded a

118

little like that of Mr. Gleason, her school's principal, only snootier. Danielle tried to keep her emotions under control.

"I'm sorry, Mr. Sweet. I never planned…"

"I'm sure you didn't," the man broke in huffily.

"Please, you have to believe me."

"Really?"

"Really. I mean, I'm really, really, *really* sorry."

Pull yourself together, Danielle told herself. *You're sounding like an idiot.* And this was such an important phone call. But no matter how she tried, the only words that seemed to come out of her mouth were "I'm sorry." She was too angry and frustrated to think straight.

"Sorry doesn't get me my horse back, Ms. Conners. You're lucky that I have indulged your parents this far about not involving the authorities, but now I must insist that you return…"

My horse. The words rattled around inside her brain like Ping-Pong balls.

"But you don't understand," Danielle pleaded. "Redman is *my* horse. Really. I'm sorry, but he's just…mine." *This is turning into a complete disaster,* she thought.

"Oh, is that so?" Mr. Sweet's voice was cool.

"Please try to understand, sir. Please. Can't I buy him back from you? We'll give you your money back and…"

"This has gone on far enough," Mr. Sweet said impatiently. "All of the arrangements have already been made. My camp will be opening soon, and we're short on suitable horses for the youngsters as it is. No, I'm afraid your suggestion is completely out of the question."

There was a moment of silence on the line. Danielle didn't know what to say next. *Well,* she told herself, *at least I tried.*

"I'll expect you and Redman within the hour," Mr. Sweet continued. "Agreed?"

"Yes, sir," Danielle said weakly.

"Good. And please be assured that if there is any further delay…"

"There won't be, sir."

"Fine. Then I won't have to call the police."

"We'll be right there, Mr. Sweet." Danielle's dad appeared at the doorway and made a sign that he wanted to speak with Mr. Sweet. "Hang on a second, sir. My dad wants to say something." She handed her dad the phone and walked outside.

Danielle sat down on the porch and stared up at the sky. It looked as if her dream of keeping Redman was utterly hopeless. She would never get her horse back from this man. But she couldn't help wondering if what Sweet had said was really true. Did he really need Redman, or was he just plain mad at her? Not that she could blame him, really. But still...

Later, out in the paddock, Danielle set to work carefully brushing and grooming her horse one last time. She'd found Redman only to lose him again. She looked into his chestnut eyes and sighed. Well, there was no getting out of it this time. "Sorry, boy," she said. "We sure tried."

In the next stall Prima was finishing up her lunch of hay and grain. Little Buddy stood beside her and squealed, impatiently waiting for his mama to give her attention to him. Danielle watched them for a moment and smiled.

She heard a noise behind her and turned to see Alec standing there. "Alec!"

"Hey, Danielle." Alec was holding half a sandwich and offered her a bite. "Did you get anything to eat yet?"

Danielle shook her head. "Just a soda. Where's the Black?

"I turned him loose in the upper pasture. He likes it there."

Danielle smiled. "I heard about the deal you made with Mom and Dad. That's great!"

Alec nodded. "Yeah, sharing the lease works out fine for me."

"I'm really sorry for what I said before." Danielle

confessed. "I feel so stupid. Please don't think I'm always like that."

"Don't be silly, Danielle. Like I said before, I'm not trying to chase you guys away. As long as I can use the barn, paddock, and pastures, I'll be happy."

"You really won't mind living next door to a jerk like me?"

Alec laughed. "Hey, I'm happy in the Coop. It's sort of cozy there. And taking care of that big old house of yours right now would be a headache for me. Like I told your mom and dad, I won't be here a lot of the time anyway. I don't know what'll happen in the future, but in the meantime, I'm sure we can all get along."

What a great guy, Danielle thought. *Boy, was I wrong about him.* Actually, she'd been wrong about a lot of things lately.

"So I hear you spoke with Mr. Sweet," Alec said. "Any luck?"

Danielle shook her head slowly. "He wouldn't even think about it."

Alec ate the last of his sandwich and watched as Danielle finished brushing out Redman's mane and tail. "I can't help you with Redman," he said finally, "but maybe you can help me with Prima and Little Buddy. The colt will be needing a lot of care and attention for the next few months. The more we work with him now, the easier it'll be for us later on.

So how would you like an after-school job? It wouldn't be very glamorous, more like mucking stalls and pitching hay, or pay much, but..." This was too good to be true. "Really?" Danielle asked eagerly. "You mean it? That's something I'd do for free."

Alec laughed. "That's okay. We'll talk about the money later. In the meantime, when you're missing Redman, remember that you're gaining a couple of new horses to help look after. Little Buddy really needs you. And if you think about it, maybe you might need him, too."

"That sounds great. Thanks, Alec," Danielle said. "I can't think of anything I'd like to do more. I really mean it."

They both looked over to where Prima was suckling her colt. It was true, Danielle thought. She'd never been around a horse this age before. It would be a challenge to take him under her wing and watch him grow. Even Redman had turned a watchful, protective eye on the little colt.

Danielle *was* incredibly grateful for all Alec was doing. Yet inside, she was torn, thinking of Little Buddy and Redman, and feeling totally mixed up. So much had happened so fast. Find Redman, lose Redman, move to the Coast, then stay, and now a new job working for Alec Ramsay. It was making her head spin.

Alec walked with Danielle and Redman to the horse trailer hitched behind Mrs. Conners's pickup.

"Just remember to keep your head up, Danielle," Alec said. "Everything's going to be okay. Deal with your problems and go on. It's the best you can do." He shook his head. "It's *all* you can do."

Danielle nodded in agreement. This time Alec's advice seemed to be more than empty words. Anyway, she appreciated the fact that he was being so supportive. And it wasn't as though he was just feeling sorry for her, Danielle thought. It was as if he actually liked her. Maybe he saw something of himself, and his love for the Black, in her affection for Redman. Redman and the Black were about as different as two horses could be, but when it came to the way their human friends felt about them, things were much the same.

Redman loaded easily, and a few minutes later Danielle and her parents were on their way to Albritton and the Sweet ranch. The three of them rode in silence. For something to do, Danielle fumbled with the radio dial until her mom told her to stop.

When they arrived at the Sweets', Danielle only half recognized the place from the night before. In the daylight it looked even bigger and more imposing.

A blond girl about fifteen years old met them at

the barn. She was wearing designer jeans, a white, long-sleeved man's dress shirt and ankle-high riding boots. Danielle immediately recognized her from the pictures she'd seen in the barn: Carol Sweet.

A stable hand in a baseball cap took Danielle's mom and dad to find Mr. Sweet. Carol stayed behind with Danielle and Redman. Danielle couldn't help feeling a bit nervous and wary of the older girl. Carol certainly hadn't seemed very nice when they'd talked on the phone.

After the grown-ups left, Carol turned to Danielle. "So you're Danielle Conners."

Who do you think I am? Danielle wanted to say. Instead, she nodded. "I talked with you on the phone, remember?" she said stiffly. "About my horse." She put a little extra emphasis on the word "my."

"Yeah, I remember," said Carol. "You hung up on me."

Danielle frowned. "No, I didn't. You cut me off."

Carol shook her head. "It must have been an accident. So why didn't you call back?"

Danielle shrugged. "It's a long story."

Carol looked Danielle up and down. Then, to Danielle's surprise, she chuckled in a friendly way. "Well, you have guts, anyway. I haven't seen my dad so mad in a real long time. How *did* you get here last night?"

Danielle wished that this girl would stop asking all these questions. What did Mr. Sweet's daughter care, anyway?

"Well, I took a bus, than I walked some..." she began.

"In all that rain?"

Danielle studied Carol's face. The older girl sure didn't seem like the snobby type she had expected. She looked genuinely interested. But why would someone like Carol Sweet care about her?

Carol reached up, gave Redman a pat, and started scratching behind his ears. "He loves to be scratched there," Danielle said.

Carol smiled. "A lot of horses do. Or else they hate it. I'll never understand why so many horses are sensitive about their ears. Do you think the Black likes to have his ears scratched?"

Danielle shrugged. "I have no idea."

"Is it true that one of his colts is staying at your place?" Carol asked. "And that Alec Ramsay is living there, too?"

"It's true," Danielle said, nodding. She told her about the new job working with Alec.

"That'll be really exciting," Carol said. "I wish *I* had an opportunity like that. The Black's colt... Wow. I'd kill to be around a horse like that. And Alec Ramsay's pretty cute, too."

Danielle raised her eyebrows. "Yeah, he's okay,"

she said. "Actually, he's been really nice."

In a way, it made Danielle feel better to have an older girl, especially one who seemed to have so much, actually envying *her*.

"So do you think your dad will ever get over being so, uh…angry?" she asked after a while. "I feel like he's trying to teach me a lesson or something."

A light smile creased the edges of Carol's eyes. "He probably is. Dad's like that sometimes. He does it to me, too. But he means well. Don't let him upset you."

"It's just that Redman and I have always been together," Danielle said. "We're *supposed* to be together, I'm sure of it. Splitting us up like this isn't right."

"Hey, let me work on him awhile," Carol said sympathetically. "I'm not promising anything, but maybe we can figure something out."

Danielle's voice quavered slightly. "Really?"

"Sure. Daddy's not so bad. He has a temper, that's all. And he's pretty stubborn, too. I know how you feel about Redman. I'd hate to have anyone try to take Mimosa away from me."

The lanky stable hand came back. He and Danielle walked Redman to an empty paddock on the other side of the barn. Carol waited by the van.

Danielle felt a bit braver this time. She tried to keep her good-bye to Redman as fast and painless as possible. She threw her arms around his neck. "I'll get you back," Danielle whispered in her horse's ear. "Somehow, some way, our luck has to change. Just hang on, Redman. I won't give up. Not ever. We'll be together again. I promise."

After a few long moments Danielle turned and walked stiffly away from the paddock, looking straight ahead. This wasn't going to be the end, she told herself. It couldn't be.

Danielle continued along the side of the freshly painted barn. Once again she noticed how immaculately kept the stable was, with everything in its proper place. The paddocks looked more like lawns than any ring she'd ever seen.

To distract herself from thinking about Redman, Danielle tried to concentrate on all the work she'd be doing with Prima and the colt. A kid could hardly ask for a better job. She told herself she should start appreciating all the breaks she'd been getting and look on the bright side of things for a change. But somehow her heart just wasn't in it.

As Danielle came around the corner of the barn and started back to the truck, her spirits sank even further. Mr. Sweet and her parents had joined Carol by the empty trailer. The blond girl was waving her hands in a rapid-fire conversation with her father. Then Mr. Sweet turned to Danielle's dad, who nodded emphatically. Danielle swallowed nervously. They were too far away for her to hear what they were saying. Undoubtedly, they all were talking about her.

When Danielle came up, Mr. Sweet shook hands with her parents and gave her a nod. Then he turned on his boot heels and walked back to the house. *What was going on?* Danielle wondered. No one was actually smiling, but Carol gave Danielle a faint, conspiratorial nod as she said good-bye and followed her dad up the walk. Mr. Conners waved Danielle toward the truck.

"Get in, Danielle."

She slid onto the middle of the seat, between her parents. They drove down the long driveway in silence.

Danielle tried to keep her mouth shut, but she finally gave up. "Okay. What were you guys talking about with Mr. Sweet?"

"Well, Carol is trying to convince her father to sell Redman back to you, that's what," Danielle's mom said quietly. "And she sounds like a very persuasive young woman, I'd say."

"Really? You mean you think there's a chance he might change his mind?"

Danielle's dad chuckled. "Not right away, maybe, but under certain conditions I think he'll go for it. That Carol should be a lawyer when she grows up."

"Conditions?" Danielle said suspiciously. "Like what?"

"Like your coming up with the money on your own, for one thing. Mr. Sweet seems to be under the impression that you need a lesson in responsibility."

Danielle grumbled under her breath. She was about to say something rude about Mr. Sweet but then wisely decided to keep her opinions to herself.

Her mom raised an eyebrow. "What was that, young lady?"

"Nothing, Mom."

"I hope not," Mrs. Conners said, "especially after what you put that man through this morning."

Danielle shrank down in her seat. "I know, Mom. I'm sorry." They rode in silence for another mile, and then Danielle turned to her dad again. "So he really said that if I come up with the money on my own I can buy Redman back?"

"That's the plan Carol is suggesting. I'd say it's pretty fair, considering."

"Did Mr. Sweet say how much?"

"Oh, somewhere in the neighborhood of a thousand dollars."

"Alec said he'd pay me for helping out with Prima and Little Buddy," Danielle said. "And maybe I can get some baby-sitting jobs."

"You do understand that money is still going to be tight for us, Danielle," her dad warned her. "You'll be needing money for things beside your horse. I'm afraid you're not going to be able to count on much of an allowance from your mother and me."

"I know, Dad," Danielle said. She sighed. "With my luck, I'll get the money together for Redman just in time for us to sell the house."

"It's possible," Mrs. Conners admitted. "Whatever Alec ends up paying you, I doubt you'll make a thousand dollars anytime soon."

"But work hard, save your money, and you'll get there," Mr. Conners said.

Danielle frowned. "A thousand dollars is twice what Mr. Sweet paid you for Redman. Why don't I have to pay him five hundred?"

"Honey, listen," Mr. Conners said. "Redman is still going to North Carolina. You'll have to pay someone to haul him back down here when you get your cash together."

"And we don't even know for sure that Mr. Sweet will go for this whole deal yet," Mrs. Conners cautioned gently.

"He *has* to," Danielle said firmly.

"I think he will," Mr. Conners said. "If I were a betting man, I'd put my money on that daughter of his. You have yourself quite a friend there, Danielle."

Danielle leaned back in her seat. It was true.

Alec Ramsay and Carol Sweet had turned out to be her friends. Her first impressions of them certainly had been wrong. And now she at least had a goal to shoot for.

The truck continued down the road to Albritton. Behind them, the empty horse trailer rattled along, sounding a little less forlorn to Danielle than it had a minute before. She gazed through the windshield. Outside, the late afternoon sun was shining brightly over the orange groves and cow pastures.

Whatever happened, Danielle vowed, one thing was certain. She had given her word to Redman to bring him back.

And that was one promise she intended to keep.

Lost and Found

Danielle walked through the front door of the Goodwill store in Albritton just before closing time. In her hand was the cash she had found inside the jacket the night before. She headed straight to the counter to turn in the money.

The gray-haired ladies behind the counter were understanding when Danielle told them the story. "Anyway, it's all here," Danielle finished. "Even the ten dollars I paid the taxi driver. I replaced that with some money I've been saving." *Now no one can say I kept one cent of that money,* she added to herself. *All it's ever done is cause me trouble.*

"That's very commendable, dear," the lady behind the register said, smiling. "You are doing the right thing. That should make you feel better, at least. We'll hold the money awhile, put a notice in the paper, and see if someone claims it."

Danielle nodded. "That sounds like a good idea."

"But there *is* something you could do for us, if you please," added the other lady. "We'll need some way for the owner to identify himself. Do you think you could go into the back room and point out the jacket you found the money in?"

"Sure," Danielle said. She made her way behind a curtain to the back room. There she found a table with the previous night's unsorted donations. She recognized a pair of pink polyester pants and a red dress with a big yellow flower on it. It took a minute or two of digging through the clothes heap, but finally she picked out the money jacket. She brought it up to the counter and left it with the ladies.

"I guess that's it, then," Danielle said, starting for the door. "Thanks again for being so nice."

"Not at all," said the lady behind the register. "Thank *you* for bringing this matter to our attention. And I wouldn't be surprised if the rightful owner gives you a reward when he or she appears. Ten percent in a case like this, wouldn't you say, Edith?"

The other gray-haired lady nodded. "Oh, yes. A reward. I should say so."

That'd be great, Danielle thought. But she wasn't going to hold her breath.

On the way out, Danielle joined her mom, who was browsing at the jewelry display case. Mrs. Conners pointed to a shiny, U-shaped pin. "Don't you have something like that, honey?"

There, in the upper-right corner of the case, was a pin that looked just like her golden horseshoe pin, the one she'd lost the night before!

Danielle peered through the glass more closely. It didn't just look like her pin. It *was* her pin.

"My lucky horseshoe!" gasped Danielle. "That's it! How did it get here?" She began hopping gleefully around the shop. Her mom looked at her suspiciously.

"It must have come loose when I was moving around inside the Goodwill box," Danielle explained. She reached down to her pockets. "Uh-oh. I don't have any money left."

Mrs. Conners sighed and started digging in her purse for her wallet when one of the gray-haired ladies came up and put her hand on Mrs. Conners's arm. "Why don't you just take the pin as a reward for being so honest and bringing the money back?" she said.

"Really?" Danielle said eagerly. "Gee, thanks!" Her mother raised one eyebrow.

"Um, to be really honest," Danielle confessed, "bringing the money back wasn't all my idea."

"Oh, I'm sure you would have done the right thing, my dear," the lady said. "Besides, I gather this pin belongs to you, anyway. Take it."

A moment later, Danielle was fastening the pin on her sweater. As she walked out of the store, feeling slightly dazed, she made sure the horseshoe was facing up.

Finding her pin after she'd returned the money might have been a coincidence, Danielle thought. But somehow she felt it was a sign her luck was changing for the better again. Now she was more certain than ever that if she worked hard and saved her money, Redman could come home in no time at all. Things could be just as they were—even better, with Alec Ramsay and his horses staying at the farm and her new friend Carol Sweet.

She touched the horseshoe pin on her jacket and smiled to herself. Some good had actually come out of this mess, after all.

Practically skipping up the empty sidewalk, Danielle hummed the melody to a song her grandma used to sing to her when she was little.

Found a horseshoe, found a horseshoe,
Picked it up and nailed it o'r the door.
It was rusty and full of nail holes,
Good luck come to me forevermore.

Danielle knew she'd bring Redman home someday soon. Very soon. But right now she couldn't wait to get back to Wishing Wells. Alec and the little colt needed her. And she needed them, too.

Things were finally starting to look up.

About the Author

Steven Farley is the son of the late Walter Farley, the man who started the tradition with the best-loved horse story of all time, *The Black Stallion*.

A freelance writer based in Manhattan, Steven Farley travels frequently, especially to places where he can enjoy riding, diving, and surfing. Along with the *Young Black Stallion* series, Mr. Farley has written *The Black Stallion's Shadow*, *The Black Stallion's Steeplechaser*, and *The Young Black Stallion*, a collaborative effort with his father.